Discard

BROTHER

BROTHER

DAVID
CHARIANDY

BROTHER

DAVID
CHARIANDY

BLOOMSBURY PUBLISHING
LONDON • OXFORD • NEW YORK • NEW DELHI • SYDNEY

BLOOMSBURY PUBLISHING
Bloomsbury Publishing Plc
50 Bedford Square, London, WC1B 3DP, UK

BLOOMSBURY, BLOOMSBURY PUBLISHING and the Diana logo
are trademarks of Bloomsbury Publishing Plc

First published in 2017 in Canada by McClelland & Stewart, Toronto
First published in Great Britain 2018

A catalogue record for this book is available from the British Library

ISBN: HB: 978-1-4088-9726-3; eBook: 978-1-4088-9729-4

2 4 6 8 10 9 7 5 3 1

Typeset by Van Dijck, by M&S Toronto
Printed and bound in Great Britain by CPI Group (UK) Ltd, Croydon CR0 4YY

To find out more about our authors and books visit www.bloomsbury.com
and sign up for our newsletters

For Austin

BROTHER

Once he showed me his place in the sky. That hydro pole in a parking lot all weed-broke and abandoned. Looking up, you'd see the dangers of the climb. The feeder lines on insulators, the wired bucket called a pole-pig, the footholds rusted bad and going way into a sky cut hard by live cables. You'd hear the electricity as you moved higher, he warned me. Feel it shivering your teeth and lighting a whole city of fear inside your head. But if you made it to the top, he said, you were good. All that free air and seeing. The streets below suddenly patterns you could read.

A great lookout, my brother told me. One of the best in the neighbourhood, but step badly on a line, touch your hand to the wrong metal part while you're brushing up against another, and you'd burn. Hang scarecrow-stiff and smoking in the air, dead black sight for all. "You want to go out like that?" he asked. So when you climbed, he said, you had to go careful. You had to watch your older brother and follow close his moves. You had to think back on every step before you took it. Remembering hard the whole way up.

He taught me that, my older brother. Memory's got nothing to do with the old and grey and faraway gone. Memory's the muscle sting of now. A kid reaching brave in the skull hum of power.

"And if you can't memory right," he said, "you lose."

ONE

She's come back. The bus pulling away from a rotting bank of snow to show her standing on the other side of the avenue. A neighbourhood girl no longer, a young woman now in heeled boots and a coat belted tight against the cold and dark. She's carrying a backpack, not a suitcase, and this really is how she becomes Aisha. The way she shoulders her belongings with a rough and impatient gesture before stepping onto the asphalt and crossing the salt-stained lanes between us.

"You're not dressed for this weather," she says.

"I'm okay. Just a short wait. You look good, Aisha."

She frowns but accepts from me a hug that lingers before we break apart and begin walking eastward, our chins hunched down against the wind tunnelling between the surrounding apartment towers. An oncoming car shocks bright her face and it's true, she does look good. The same dark skin haunted with red, the same hair she once scorned as "mongrel." But it's been ten years since last we've spoken. And in the silence thick between us it feels like even the smallest dishonesty will ruin this reconnection. A truck blasts suddenly past us on the avenue, spraying slush on our pant legs and shoes. Aisha swears, but when our eyes meet she offers a thin smile.

"Properly welcomed back," she says.

"You do look a bit tired. I've made a bed for you."

"Thank you, Michael. Thank you for offering me a place to stay. I'm sorry for not saying so sooner. My head these days. And you know me, I've never been good with favours."

She was overseas when she got the news that her father had been admitted into intensive care, and during her phone call to me she described how her mind instantly filled with panic but also vague anger. In his occasional letters to her, he had mentioned that he was feeling tired, but he had not admitted the cancer. She caught a long series of connecting flights to Toronto, and then a Greyhound bus to the hospice in Milton, the small town he had moved to only recently. She stayed with him for the week until the end, and there had been time to talk but not nearly enough. "What was there to say?" she asked me in a rough voice over the phone, the line hanging afterwards with a quiet impossible for me to fill. This call out of nowhere. "Please visit," I said to her, doubt creeping into my voice even as I repeated myself. "Come home to the Park."

The Park is all of this surrounding us. This cluster of low-rises and townhomes and leaning concrete apartment towers set tonight against a sky dull purple with the wasted light of a city. We are approaching the western edge of the Lawrence Avenue bridge, a monster of reinforced concrete over two hundred yards in length. Hundreds of feet beneath it runs the Rouge Valley, cutting its own way through the suburb, heedless of man-made grids. But the Rouge is invisible to us tonight, and we have just arrived at the Waldorf, a townhouse complex at the edge of the bridge and made of crumbling salmon brick, flapping blue tarps draped eternally over its northeast corner. The unit where Aisha lived ten years ago with her father is on the prized south of the building, away from traffic. But the side where I have remained all my life is at the busy edge of the avenue, exposed to the constant hiss of tires on asphalt. I warn Aisha about the loose concrete on the doorsteps and suffer a sudden bout of clumsiness working the brass key into the lock. I push open the door to show a living room lit blue with the shifting light of a television, its volume turned off. There is a couch with its back towards us, and on it there is a woman with greying hair who does not turn.

I gesture to Aisha that we should be quiet. I remove my shoes in a demonstrating way, and with our coats still on I quickly guide Aisha across the living room. The woman on the couch continues to watch the silent television, the mime of a talk-show interview, a celebrity guest throwing his head back in laughter. I lead Aisha down a short hallway to the second bedroom. A small lamp casting a circle of light upon a desk, a bunk bed with a mattress and sheets on the lower bed only, the upper bunk long ago stripped bare, even the mattress removed, leaving skeletal slats of wood. I close the door behind us and in the sudden smallness of the room begin explaining. We won't be sleeping together on the bed, of course. I'll be using the living room couch, which is quite comfortable, honestly. I point out the towel and extra blankets set out very obviously on the sheets of the lower bunk. I stop when I notice that Aisha is staring and that she hasn't let her backpack touch the floor.

"Your mother doesn't speak anymore?" she asks.

"She speaks. She's just quiet sometimes, especially at night."

"I'm sorry," she says to me, shaking her head. "I shouldn't have come. This is an intrusion."

Bullets of slush smattering upon the bedroom window. Another truck that has passed too close to the curb outside. But in the wake of sudden noise, a feeling creeps upon me, one of shame, maybe, for imagining that I could try to end our conversation tonight like this. With talk of sleeping arrangements and towels. With acknowledgement of Aisha's father, yet no acknowledgement of that other loss shadowing this room and measured in the ten years of silence between us.

"I still think of Francis," she says.

FRANCIS WAS MY OLDER BROTHER. His was a name a toughened kid might boast of knowing, or a name a parent might pronounce in warning. But before all of this, he was the shoulder pressed against me bare and warm, that body always just a skin away.

Our mother had come from Trinidad, in what parents of her generation called the West Indies. It was a place that Francis and I, both born and raised here in Canada, had visited once and could recognize vaguely in words and sounds and tastes. It was a place that accounted for the presence in our house of certain drinks like mauby and sorrel and also the inexplicably named Peardrax, which Francis had once fooled me into believing was bathroom cleanser. Somehow, we felt that the West Indies made sense of other equally strange objects in our home, like the snow globe of Niagara Falls, or the lurking threat of Anne Murray's "Snowbird" 45. It was a place populated by relatives we had met only briefly, who existed now in old black-and-white photographs, ghostly images that were supposed to explain our eyes and way of smiling, our hair and bones.

There was another old photograph in the house, one that Francis discovered when we were small, shelved secretly in Mother's bedroom cupboard. It showed a man with a moustache groomed so carefully it looked painted on. He wore a thin light-coloured jacket, the open collar of his shirt slightly kinked up. Old words like *suave* and *debonair* came to mind, or at least they do now. This man was our father, who was also from the West Indies, and who now lived somewhere in the city, although he had left our home when Francis was three and I was only two. The photograph wasn't perfectly focused, and I remember Francis and me as children looking hard into the blur of the man's face for something recognizable. His skin was much darker than Mother's, but we had been told that he was not black like her, but something called "Indian"—although this identity seemed lost in the poorness of the photograph, or in the trowel-thick application of Brylcreem in his hair, as artificial as the black snap-on do of Lego Man.

In truth, none of us, not me, Francis, or Mother, had much interest in the grey pasts of photographs. We had more than enough to explore right here and now, and most of all we had the running challenge of what our mother called "opportunity." Mother worked as a cleaner in office buildings and malls and hospitals. She was also one of *those* black mothers, unwilling to either seek or accept help from others. Unwilling to suffer any small blow to her sense of independence or her vision of eventual arrival. And so if a job suddenly arose in some distant part of the city but held the promise of future opportunities, or if, just as suddenly, the opportunity for time-and-a-half beckoned, she would accept the work, though it meant leaving her two young boys alone at home.

She was never happy about abandoning us, and if she learned the evening before of an impending night shift, she would spend precious sleep time cooking and worrying over the details of meals and activities for the following day. If we had homework, she would set it out on the dining room table beside plates of cook-up and greens, or rice and stew chicken. There was tenderness in the dishes she prepared, love in a dish made perfect with the fruity bite of Scotch bonnet. But by the time she started putting on her coat and shoes, she would be in a state, exhausted, almost overcome with guilt, yet expressing it in bitter scoldings and fantastic threats. Her voice, schooled harshly in the Queen's English, now articulating threats mined from the deepest hells of history.

"No answering the door or turning up the heat. No turning on the oven or stovetop at any time. You hear me, Francis? I will strap your backside *red* if I come back to find you or your brother hurt. *Absolutely* no TV after eight if I'm not back until then. No *A-Team* or Mrs. T or any other gangster foolishness in my home. Oh you smiling now? You think is joke? You feel you too *harden* to listen to me? Then you both go right ahead and touch that stove dial. Just answer that front door once. I will string you up by your thumbnails from the ceiling. I will skin you alive and screaming. I will beat you so hard your *children* will bear scars. Your children's *children* will feel!"

Francis and I would nod and shake our heads all at once in urgent promising. Mother would neat up her uniform and hair in the mirror by the door and then leave without looking back, locking the door and testing the doorknob several times before we heard faintly among the noise of traffic her feet clopping quickly away on the sidewalk. In the hours that followed, Francis and I would try to be good. We would eat our dinner and put away the dishes and only afterwards find high up in the kitchen cupboards the other tastes we craved. Thick mouthfuls of corn syrup sucked direct from the yellow beehive container. The tongue-stinging green of Jell-O powder licked slowly from a spoon. We'd do the homework Mother had laid out for us, but, later, we'd learn equally important life skills and facts about the world from *Three's Company* and *The Dukes of Hazzard*. When we were a bit older, on those Friday nights when Mother was away we'd watch late-night Italian comedies with the enticing parental guidance warnings. Francis and I each suffering patiently through intricate plots in a foreign language for the promise of a couple seconds of boob.

"They're showing!" he once shouted from the living room. "*Both* of them at once! You have to get here now! Right now!"

"Wait! Wait!" I called from the bathroom. Stumbling, falling, then crawling with my pants still around my ankles until I reached him and could see. But *nothing*. Only that late-night infomercial for the Ronco food dehydrator.

Francis's laughter. Stupid beef jerky.

In every case, he would have the decency and respect to wait for at least an hour before making his move. And the first time Mother left us alone, it was magic. When the sun had begun to set, my brother dragged a chair from the kitchen to reach the deadbolt on the front door. He clicked the lock open, and pushed at the door, and here it was before us. The freedom of Lawrence Avenue. Security lights and rust-stained apartment buildings.

"Remember," Francis told me. "We never answered the front door."

The world around us was named Scarborough. It had once been called "Scarberia," a wasteland on the outskirts of a sprawling city. But now, as we were growing up in the early '80s, in the heated language of a changing nation, we heard it called other names: Scarlem, Scarbistan. We lived in Scar-*bro*, a suburb that had mushroomed up and yellowed, browned, and blackened into life. Our neighbours were Mrs. Chandrasekar and Mr. Chow, Pilar Fernandez and Clive "Sonny" Barrington. They spoke different languages, they ate different foods, but they were all from one colony or the other, and so they had a shared vocabulary for describing feral children like us. We were "ragamuffins." We were "hooligans" up to no good "gallivanting." We were what one neighbour, more poet than security guard, described as "oiled creatures of mongoose cunning," raiding dumpsters and garbage rooms or climbing up trees and fire-exit stairs to spy on adults. During winters we snowballed cars on Lawrence Avenue, dipping into the back alleys if the drivers tried to pursue us. A Pinto Wagon once shaving past my face, its wake tugging hard upon my body, Francis's hand upon my shoulder pulling me safe.

During the day, we had more formal educational opportunities. Our school was named after Sir Alexander Campbell, a Father of Confederation. But we the students of his school had our own confederations, our own schoolyard territories and alliances, our own trade agreements and anthems. We listened to Planet Rock and carried Adidas bags and wore stonewashed jeans and painter caps. You could hear us whenever there were general assemblies in the auditorium, our collective voices overwhelming whatever politely seated ceremony we were supposed to be attending.

Hey Francis, homeboy, my man.

Rudebwoy Francis! Gangstar!

Francis and I each served out long sentences in classrooms beneath the chemical hum of white fluorescent lights, in part out of fear of our mother, who warned us, upon pain of something worse than death, not to squander "our only chance." But Francis actually liked to learn. He read books, and he was a good observer.

And after class was out there were other institutions to learn from. A dozen blocks west of the towers and housing complexes of the Park, at the intersection of Markham and Lawrence, there lay a series of strip malls. There were grocery shops selling spices and herbs under signs in foreign languages and scripts, vegetables and fruits with vaguely familiar names like ackee and eddo. There were restaurants with an average expiry date of a year, their hand-painted signs promising ice cream with the "back home tastes" of mango and khoya and badam kulfi, a second sign written urgently in red marker promising that they'd also serve, whenever asked, the mystery of "Canadian food."

Also the Heritage Value convenience store, run by that asshole who framed his useless foreign degree, despised the dark stinking guts of every other immigrant, and bullied his wife and two daughters into endless hours at the cash register, advertising lottery tickets and low phone rates to Kingston and Saigon and Colombo and Port of Spain. The father hated Francis and me, recognizing the look of "no money" on our faces. We had little chance of sneaking into his store when he was working. But if his wife or daughters were on shift, we might slip in and buy a few singles of Double Bubble and maybe a pack of three-flavoured Fun Dip. We'd scope out the freezer section with its Klondike Bars and Eskimo Pies frosted thick with crystals, their prices always out of reach. We might even be allowed to steal a few moments at the comic book display, pretending to debate a buy but actually reading as quickly as possible. Those stories of heroes masked and misread. Their secret origins, their endless war with darkest evil.

Francis had nightmares. He'd be lying in the bunk above me, and I'd listen to his breathing, the soft wheeze he might have from allergies or a cold. He'd be on the edge of sleep when some terror would visit him. He'd wake screaming a deep body scream, all cracked throat and emptied stomach, and it would take me a while to realize that I'd been screaming too. If Mother was home, she'd offer comfort. She'd lie beside us, and with the warmth of her body push back the fear. We'd lie quiet and awake, the three of us, for a long time, watching the wind blow ghosts into the drapes and cars passing by on the avenue cast moving lights upon the walls and ceiling.

Never speaking. Listening for things.

What scares two boys aged ten and eleven? Sometimes, in the midst of our play, a siren would cut the air and cars with flashing lights would brake screeching on the avenue, a neighbourhood kid soon cuffed on the sidewalk, his face turned away from us in shame. There were tales about boys jumped and beaten, faces ruined, jaws wired shut. "I saw it myself," claimed one; "I *did* it," claimed another, and we were never sure if either ought to be believed. Always, there were stories on TV and in the papers of gangs, killings in bad neighbourhoods, predators roaming close. One morning, I peered with Francis into a news-paper box to read a headline about the latest terror and caught in the glass the reflection of our own faces.

From the age of seven, Francis could read. He read books, of course, regularly and well into his teens. But he could also read the many signs and gestures around us. He could read the faces of the neighbourhood youth hanging around outside 7-Eleven and know when to offer a nod or else a sly joke or else just to keep moving and not just then attempt to meet a bruised pair of eyes. But especially, Francis could read our mother. He recognized her pride, but also the routes and tolls of her labours. He knew that for work as a cleaner, and sometimes a nanny, she had not only tough hours but also long journeys, complicated rides along bus routes to faraway office buildings and malls and homes, long waits at odd hours at stops and stations, sometimes in the rain or the thick heat of the afternoon, sometimes in the cold and dark of winter. He understood that there is a specific moment during the trip back home from work when a mother's body threatens to give out. A specific site in the bus loop at Kennedy Station when exhaustion closes in and the limbs feel like meat, and it takes every last strength from a mother to make the two additional bus transfers home.

When Francis was still not quite a teen, and Mother returned home in a state, he would go to work. He would casually offer her a cool, damp cloth for her head, maybe even a pan of water and Epsom salts for her feet. He would fetch a blanket in winter, or a fan and a glass of water in summer. He was careful never to overdo his concern, and so wound her pride, or otherwise to break any of the household rules she had established to help us through lean times. But one hot summer day, when Mother collapsed on the couch, shaking her head at all offered food, unwilling to take a sip of water or even to open her eyes, twelve-year-old Francis dared big.

He went to the kitchen and took from the freezer a can of orange juice concentrate. We had been warned repeatedly by Mother never to touch such stuff without her permission. And if she allowed us to touch it, we were to use five cans of water to dilute the concentrate, never three as the fool instructions on the can said. But on that day, Francis used just one can of water, mashing it into the frozen lump of concentrate with a wooden spoon, and pouring the slush bright into a glass. He gently lowered the glass into Mother's curled fingers, her eyes still closed. I braced for all hell to break loose as she tasted, her mouth moving as if eating pudding.

"I made it sweet this time," explained Francis.

"*Sweet*," Mom said, a tired smile.

She touched his face. She cupped his chin and touched the growing shadow of his moustache. She pinched his earlobe lightly between her thumb and finger as if it were a raindrop from a leaf, then reached to gently pluck something from his hair. A burr from the Rouge Valley.

The Rouge Valley. It was a wound in the earth. A scar of green running through our neighbourhood, hundreds of feet deep in some places, a glacial valley that existed long before anything called Scarborough. It had been bridged near our home, turned into a park with a paved asphalt walkway running alongside the creek. When we were very young, and Mother could spare the time, she would take us there for picnics. But soon Francis and I preferred to visit it on our own, scorning the paved walkway down into its parklands, opting instead for the footpath that we ourselves had broken through the undergrowth and down the steep slope until we reached the floor of that deep green valley.

When we were very young, we'd build forts and hideaways in the brush, using branches but also cardboard and broken pieces of furniture occasionally dumped here. We'd race twigs in the creek, spot the little speckled fish swimming together in the blowing current, hunt for the other small lives that had managed to survive in the park unnoticed. The tracks in the mud of a muskrat or a raccoon or maybe a turtle. One summer we used a stick to corner a crayfish, blue-red and mottled, and Francis explained shiveringly how it grew by cracking its own body open. One fall we piled the stuff of this land over our bodies like blankets. Coloured leaves and pine needles, branches and the barbed wire of thistles. Also plastic bags and foil drifting down from the fast-food joints above. Our hair camouflaged with mashed drinking straws and rushes. Our faces already the colour of earth.

The Rouge was not "nature," not that untouched land you could watch on wildlife shows or read about in history books. The Rouge wasn't the sort of place you could pretend to have discovered, nor imagine empty and now your own. But it was the place we knew, and the place, even as we grew older, we kept returning to.

Late one evening during the fall Francis turned fourteen, we visited for the last time. It had been a long time, perhaps more than a year, since we'd gone to the Rouge together. We walked to the edge of the bridge and spent a bit of time rummaging along the guardrail, trying to find the head of our path amidst the brush and fallen leaves and blown trash from the road. Twice passing cars honked angrily at us. Finally, Francis said, "Over here," and we began edging carefully down the steepest part of the valley's slope, slipping wildly and only slowing down by grabbing brush and low branches. Eventually, the ground levelled and we broke out into a small clearing. Francis had a green canvas backpack with him, and when we were seated by the creek he surprised me by pulling out a six-pack of Molson Canadian. He broke one from its plastic ring and opened it with a soft whisper crack and passed it to me. I sipped carefully, trying not to make a face at the bitterness. We were quiet for some time as we drank our cans and the trees turned to black shadows against the night sky.

When I was a child, Francis protected me. I was smaller than him, of course, but I was also somehow less of a proper presence. There was my nervous smile. There was my hair, which, unlike his, was fundamentally indecisive, forever caught in that no man's zone between Afro and hockey mullet. As I approached adolescence, there was the growing concern over my cultural tastes. My air-drumming to Rush, for instance, or my painstaking illustration of the flowing-haired Gondolfin, my fourteenth-level multi-classed half-elf, now abruptly recognized as gay. Francis and I had lived together in the same room all of our lives, but there had recently been a series of disheartening intimacies. The occasion when Francis came home with new friends and they caught me before the television imitating the dancing in Lionel Richie's "All Night Long." The far more serious time he walked into our bedroom to see me masturbating with Mazola corn oil to the women's underwear section of the Eaton's catalogue.

"Eaton's?" he had asked me later, softly, never meeting my eyes. "*Really?*"

So as we sat with our beer in the Rouge, I expected him to give me one of his lectures on conduct and attitude, on "getting it." But instead, we just helped ourselves to a second can of Canadian. We listened to the night sounds of insects and the thinned waters of the creek and the muffled noises of vehicles passing high above us on the bridge. And when Francis did speak, it was about neighbourhood boys. He mentioned Scatter and Brownman, Tiger and Anton, and I knew them all. When I was alone, in the schoolyard or strip mall parking lot, they would push me around in showy ways, never really hurting me, just humiliating me, reminding me of my place in the world. But Francis had intervened, and the targeting stopped. Francis said these very same boys talked about the disses they had experienced. They talked about lurking enemies and of protecting themselves with weapons.

"Assholes," I said.

Francis nodded, and I could tell it was not only a nod of agreement but also the gesture you make when a point has been missed and you just want to move on because it's all somehow too old and too late to try now to explain.

I know now that by the age of fourteen, you feel it. You spot the threat that is not only about young men with weapons, about "gangs" and "predators," but also the threat that is slow and somehow very old. A mother lecturing you about arrival and opportunity while her breath stinks of the tooth she can't just for the moment afford the time or money to fix. And as Francis began to approach adulthood, he grew dissatisfied with the world and with his destined place in it.

By the time Francis turned eighteen, he spent almost all his time away from me and with boys I didn't know well at all. They were older and from different parts of Scarborough, not just the Park. They styled themselves in big pants and unzipped sports jackets, loud hats and the right kinds of shoes. They wore tight fades, with cuts etched into the paint-thin hairs around the sides of their heads. They spoke and gestured in ways that asserted connections beyond Scarborough, to scenes in New York and L.A. and Kingston. They seemed to have their own language, and I'd watch very carefully when they greeted Francis by touching hands and sharing a private joke. But if I tried to worm my way into their circle, saying "sup" or maybe agreeing too eagerly on any matter ("Yeah, homeboy is indubitably *dope*!"), there'd be a difficult moment of silence when they'd look at me, and then at Francis, and then back at me, as if they couldn't understand the relationship. As if they couldn't figure out what, genetically, had gone so wrong.

"Hey," Francis would say to me. "Can you give us a little space?"

At home, he still helped Mother after work, and she would still touch his face. But increasingly the sympathies that had existed between them strained, and an unspoken irritability and tension seemed to grow with each passing day. And now, when she touched his body, it was often rough, to indicate the lack of "respectabil-ity" and "plain civilization" he signalled through hair and clothes and posture. But always the biggest fight was about school. Like me, Francis had years ago been streamed out of an academic program into a basic one. He stayed cool about the whole thing. His new-found disinterest in school perfectly countered its apparent disinterest in him. But in his last year of high school he told a teacher to fuck off, and he was expelled with threats to call the police. "Your one and only chance!" Mother repeated over and over again.

Francis never went back to school. He got a series of temporary jobs and quietly added groceries to the fridge. He worked hard to prove he wasn't frittering his life away, and he came home looking almost as worn out as our mother, yet this only irritated her more. And then, that summer, just as you could sense the heat coming, the hostility between them erupted. Mother had been taken aside by a neighbour and informed that Francis was spending all his spare time at Desirea's, a barbershop filled with boys apparently possessing records.

"Deny this!" Mother screamed. "Deny to my face that you spend time there! Deny these boys are known to police!"

Francis had long since learned not to argue directly with Mother. He appeared to listen while never perfectly meeting her eyes, and in this way acted neither foolishly aloof nor confrontational. But this time, as she stood dripping in her coat, Francis's technique didn't work. He would not ignore her, Mother warned. He would not get away with pretending nothing was happening.

"You are my *son*!" she yelled. "You will never be a *criminal*."

Maybe it was the way Mother pronounced the word, briefly stepping out of the Queen's English and into the music of her Trinidadian accent. Cri-mi-*nal*. Or maybe it was something else, some creeping sense of unfairness or inevitability. But Francis laughed. For a moment, Mother just stared. The sharp brass door key forgotten in her hand when she struck him across the face.

Silence as Francis slowly brought up his hand to touch his cheek. His eyes blinking with hurt and surprise, a thin red line welling on his skin. Until his eyes changed and he smiled. As if this, somehow, were a victory.

A month later, an enveloping heat arrived, a physical oppression from which none could escape. Nature carrying on like the sort of thug you only hear about. In the early morning it was a menacing red haze. By the afternoon it was a syrup misery in the air, suffocating your will, making even breathing difficult. Even at night there was no relief, and the heat cooked up all day within our homes made staying there unbearable. One evening Mother came back from work and went straight to her bedroom, her hair stuck with sweat to her forehead, ignoring the glass of water Francis had discreetly set out for her. After she closed the door behind her, Francis asked me to step outside to talk.

We walked to an abandoned parking lot not too far, within sight of the concrete apartment towers near our home, the MacDonald, the Scott, the ones just numbered. Some younger kids on bikes were hanging out in the parking lot. One of them raised his hand shyly towards Francis, the way a boy sometimes does to an older boy who has managed to win himself a reputation, but Francis ignored him and the kid went back to joking with his friends.

"I'm going away," Francis told me.

"What? Where? When?"

"Soon. A couple weeks, maybe. I'm working on the details."

"What about Mother?" I asked him.

"I'll tell her soon," Francis said. "She'll understand."

"But she needs your help."

"You help her out too. She'll be all right. There'll be one less mouth to feed."

"But she relies on you."

"Come on, Michael," he told me. "I wouldn't just abandon her. I'll send her money. And she's strong. She's survived stuff we don't even know about."

He breathed out and shook his head, and he looked at

the apartment towers, their darkened windows, lights kept low during the heat wave. And I remember in that moment feeling so haunted by the sight. As if through magic a whole neighbourhood had been made to disappear. As if a power existed to do such a thing.

Earlier that week, we'd heard there'd been trouble in the Park. A dispute among some young men that had amplified into a beating. Not a showy brag of a beating, a bit of roughing up with loud threats thrown in, maybe the flash of a weapon, fake or not, but a real beating. Some guy getting whaled on hard by a group of boys, his ribs broken, his fingers stomped, his hair doused with lighter fluid and set on fire, thin blue in the dark. "A halo," Anton had told us. His skin-teeth smile.

    Francis and I both knew better than to believe every fool story about our neighbourhood someone told us, even a boy like Anton, who had lately turned into a petty dealer with a small bit of real knowing. But on that night, as my brother and I returned to our block, we sharpened when we saw a bunch of guys we didn't recognize hanging out in the roundabout of our complex. They were shouting at one another. "Kill you fool." "Yeah. Step to me." Someone shouted from a balcony, "We've called the cops already. The cops are coming," but the shouting only grew louder and more threatening.

    Don't touch me, punk.

Fucking pussy. Faggot.

Yeah, nigga, you want some? You want some, bitch?

We quickened our steps and cut wide away from them. But as we turned the corner of our building, we heard it. A short bang like a car backfiring, a sound almost ordinary. We heard another bang, and then a bunch very quick after that, unmistakable, not ordinary at all. There were a few more shots around us, the sudden splintering of bricks a few yards away, a frog of asphalt leaping from the ground. We should have moved, but we didn't. Even when we heard more shots. And then from around the corner of our building footsteps running towards us. He had just turned into our view when there was another shot, and a sound like a pumpkin dropped from a balcony at Halloween, and the runner fell.

It was Anton. I could tell this from his navy blue track suit, even though his face was turned away. He was making soft animal noises and a wet pink balloon seemed to leak from his head. I began to pull away, even as Francis went closer to look. He bent over the body. He reached to touch Anton's face and then pulled his hand back as if burned.

"Francis," I whispered.

Another gunshot, but my brother didn't move. He looked at his hand, and tried to wipe something off it on to his pants. I called to him again. Then another shot, more yelling.

"Francis," I tried again.

And only when we heard the wail of a siren did he turn to me. His face shocked white in the brittle security light.

Run, he told me. No sound, just the shape of the word in his mouth.

We hadn't got very far when a cop car raced past us, followed by another that U-turned and screeched to a halt just behind us with a rubber stink. The sounds of doors opening and of commands, loud, urgent. Booted feet upon the sidewalk running towards us, and now a second feeling of terror, as if welling up from some old dark dream.

We had been stopped by the cops before. There was a routine to it all: we knew that if you carefully played along you'd eventually be released, if not with your dignity, then at least with your skin. But that night we sensed an urgency we hadn't experienced before. With the blinding headlights upon me, I couldn't process the commands. I noticed Francis with his hands behind his head, and I realized that I ought to do the same, but I couldn't. I felt a cop grab my shoulder and yank. I heard Francis say "hey" as he reached instinctively for me.

I was a poor witness to what happened next. My face was pressed down and away from Francis right from the beginning, but I could hear beside me the struggle, a sharp slap, the hollow sound of something heavy on flesh, breath pushed violently out of lungs and mouth. I was put in cuffs and lifted into a seated position. I sensed Francis was near to me, and I had to crane my neck to see him, also sitting upright with cuffed hands behind him. He had a bloody scrape on his cheekbone, and that seemed to be the worst of it. I tried silently to get him to meet my eyes, but he wouldn't.

"Francis," I whispered to him.

"Shut up," said a cop.

"*Francis*," I whispered a bit louder.

"I told you shut the fuck up."

We were lucky. Eventually, without any word from us, it was reasoned that we weren't directly involved. We were released from our cuffs and asked to sit on the side of the street. Over the next hour, we watched a train of emergency vehicles heading towards our building. Cop cars, a fire truck, three ambulances, two news vans.

Another police car stopped beside us, and an older cop with a shaven head got out to talk with the other officers. The older cop listened to the two who had cuffed us, and as he did he drew out a first and then a second stick of gum from a package and chewed. He looked completely uninterested in Francis and me, and only after listening for a good amount of time did he crouch down, breathing peppermint on us. He was offered latex gloves by one of the other cops, but he shook his head and used his bare hand to very gently coax Francis's head towards the street light so he could look at the scrape on his cheek-bone. My brother jerked his face away. The cop stood and chewed for a second longer.

"Okay," he said, "We're taking you home."

It had become almost unrecognizable. Our neighbour-hood now a crime scene cast hard in the clashing bright-ness of emergency. Cop cars with flashing lights were parked up and down the street, on empty lots and in the soft grass of courtyards, leaving long muddy tire tracks. There were two, three, four ambulances, and also the news vehicles with satellite dishes and milling reporters with microphones under bright TV lights. Illuminated, the buildings I had known all my life were changed. The stucco of a low-rise looked like the sole of an unwashed child; the rust on the balcony railings and fire exits of an apartment tower looked ugly and contagious, a bub-bling rash. Even the ordinary clothes that people hung to dry on laundry lines suddenly looked suspicious. Conspiracies in the open hanging of slacks and saris, in headless baby jumpers.

So many of our neighbours had gathered to watch, some on their balconies, others on the bright stages of courtyards and taped-off streets. A man cradled a child who wouldn't sleep. A small girl held her mom's hand, and a group of younger kids normally buzzing with annoying energy looked silently upon the scene. I'd grown up among these people. I knew their faces and family names. The Cumberbatches and Rampersads and Nowaks. They had blank expressions on their faces. Maybe from the intensity of the light, maybe because they wanted to give nothing away of themselves to others. But most looked the way you do when you're being studied unfavourably. When you're being watched but also trying to see.

But it was Mother who now sticks most in my head. As the cops walked us home, she was standing on the porch, still wearing her blue cleaner's uniform. She watched both of us approaching with the cops, but especially her eldest son, who, on this night of violence, was somehow unable to meet her eyes.

"Ma'am?" asked the cop. "Are you the mother?"

She nodded and listened but looked beyond the cops to the audience of staring neighbours. The combination of sweat and glare made her face shine like a mask, and she looked a bit like an actor who'd stumbled accidentally onto a stage and who now, too late, had to figure out her role.

TWO

For the past ten years, I've been careful with Mother. I've kept to a minimum all discomforting talk about the past. I've given away things belonging to Francis that might remind and disturb. His concert shirts and sneakers. His Blue Jays cap with its faint dried stain of sweat upon the brim.

I got rid of these items not to deny my mother the chance to remember her son but to allow us both the time and space to reckon with loss. When Francis was first gone, Mother was unable to work or move. But in the past couple years she's grown increasingly independent. She helps me cook and keep house. She has a part-time position as a cleaner at the community centre, a job that covers only a small part of our household expenses but does not require of her long hours travelling. She is the proof that those who have suffered enormous loss can also endure. She is rarely the still and staring woman before a television Aisha spotted earlier tonight. Although she does have her moments.

A few weeks ago, she left the house dressed in neat clothes appropriate for the cold weather, the right shoes and a warm hat. She wasn't gone for too long, perhaps only two or three hours, just long enough for me to begin worrying. But when she returned, I understood. She was struggling with grocery bags containing dried peas, herbs, spice powders, a cloth bag of rice, leafy greens sticking out the tops. It wasn't the heat-and-serve sort of stuff that I've admittedly too often fed her, but ingredients that you'd buy at the cluster of Sri Lankan, Filipino, and West Indian grocers a few blocks west, food you actually had to spend time preparing. And then I suddenly remembered the date. At midnight it would be Francis's birthday.

"I am going to cook," she said.

I helped her unpack the bags. Dasheen and soursop and bodi, names I had learned imperfectly throughout my childhood, in the same way I learned that "pears" are not really pears at all but avocados and that "figs" are green bananas and "breadfruit" is not bread or fruit. Mother had not cooked for a very long time, but when she got to work, she entered an old and patient rhythm, putting lentils to soak, chopping vegetables, roasting spices. She did it all with a fluency I'd thought she'd lost. There were moments of drift, though. A staring spell as a pot of rice boiled over, and then as garlic in a pan smoked and bittered. She peeled a cabbage but then continued removing leaves until nothing was left, just her panicked eyes and empty trembling hands.

"Oh," she said softly.

"It's all right, Mother."

"Oh dear."

In the end, some ingredients were left untouched, but what she had prepared was good. Rice cooked with beans and small cubes of meat with bones. A stew of bright red lentils. A dish of pale vegetables cooked slow into a deep orange richness. She set the table using the good napkins and cutlery, and I kept quiet when she set a third plate, a third glass of water with a drop of lemon juice. We ate, and we later watched the evening news, and we afterwards each went to our bedrooms for what I hoped would be a decent rest.

I was awakened by sounds from the dark living room. I stepped out of my room, not exactly worried about an intruder but filled, all the same, with fear. I found Mother in the kitchen, sitting on the floor and whispering into the phone. She was spelling out a name. "F-R-A-N-C-I-S," she explained. "Please help me reach him." She noticed me and pulled the receiver away from her ear, and I could hear the annoyed operator asking for a last name. Mother gently hung up the phone and stood before speaking.

"I understand," she told me. "I know he is gone."

I believed her. I knew that only for a moment, on the edge of sleep, my mother imagined there was a country code she could dial, a toll she could pay.

Our neighbours in the Park have witnessed spells like these too. Instances when Mother seems to drift or stare or wander into the past. Some of our neighbours have memories of the events that began with the shootings that hot summer. But new people are always arriving in the Park. And they often come under challenging circumstances, from the Caribbean, from South Asia and Africa and the Middle East, from places like Jaffna and Mogadishu. For these newer neighbours, there is always a story connected to Mother and me, a story made all the more frightening through each inventive retelling among neighbours. It is a story, effectively vague, of a young man deeply "troubled," and of a younger brother carrying "history," and of a mother showing now the creep of "madness."

Some of our neighbours avoid us outright. They offer tight hellos when we pass, and hurried footsteps if we happen to be walking in the same direction. They lean their heads together to whisper. But there are also many kind gestures. To this very day, trays of food will sometimes appear at our front door. A pilau with okra, a stew chicken unmistakably Caribbean. Sometimes the dishes are at first less familiar: a bowl of pakoras or a dish of seasoned rice marinated and wrapped in leaves. Most often, they are dropped off anonymously, placed in the kind of disposable foil trays that signal clearly that they do not need to be returned. But, occasionally, food will be delivered in Corning Ware that will have to be retrieved, and when it is there will sometimes be inquiries about the state of my mother. And this is how, only a week ago, I answered the door, yet again, to Mrs. Henry.

You have to understand Mrs. Henry. She is one of the many certified Mothers of the neighbourhood, a force, a stern uplifter of fallen individuals, especially of those parents afflicted with troublesome, wayward children. She is an elder at a nearby Pentecostal church, and she lets you know this immediately. She works most mornings at a factory that cans fish, but she wears a hat and proper full-length dress to travel there. She has three jobs, she will announce, and also a boy who sings in a choir, and none of this is special, she will tell you. This is how she was raised in the West Indies, a place she invokes against the iniquity and salacious immorality afflicting Scarborough and its youth. She is the perfect embodiment of law and respectability, dark-faced and smelling righteously of Limacol cologne, peppermint breath mints, and coconut oil pomade.

"Good evening, Mrs. Henry," I said.

You always say "good evening" to a woman like Mrs. Henry. You don't try "hello" or, worse yet, "hi," and no child of this neighbourhood, however foolish or *harden*, would ever risk anything like a "sup?" But to my proper greeting Mrs. Henry barely responded. She asked about her serving dish, and I gave it to her, washed. She asked if I had kept the fry fish out of the fridge until it cooled "lest it sweat," and I said I had, lying. I thanked her sincerely, and then, remembering my manners, suggested that she come in for tea. She gave me the look that I have often seen on the faces of neighbours. That awkward look of smell that might accompany a sense, from the air, that something lies unburied. She gave me another look too, something softer, perhaps pity.

"Another time," she said.

I do not blame my neighbours for avoiding Mother and me. They carry their own histories and their own hopes of genuine arrival. They are marked by language and religion and skin, and their jobs are often temporary and fragile. And if, for these very reasons, they sometimes display to Mother the everyday acts of kindness and generosity that come out of a deep sense of vulnerability, they also understand the costs of stigmatization, and how certain stories cling stinking to the flesh. Some neighbours, I've heard, have taken up the old practice of writing fake addresses on job applications, out of fear that acknowledging a connection to the Park will further jeopardize their already complicated lives.

But this is all right with me. I don't want others in my life. I don't want houseguests or questioning conversations. I certainly don't want more drama for Mother. Ten years has not, in fact, been yet enough time to fully recover. Though now, we do have a guest in our home.

Tonight, at least, I have avoided any needless confrontation. For the actual arrival of Aisha to our home has turned out to be less trying than I thought it would. After she spoke Francis's name, I nodded and then all but abandoned her in my room to settle in for the night. I joined Mother in the living room watching television, her eyes focused somewhere beyond the lit screen, until the beginnings of an infomercial for sunglasses, and she rose and went to her bedroom, and I was able to stretch out on the couch. Since then, I have been kept awake by the hiss of passing cars.

And now, on the edge of sleep, the shootings return to me with an attack of panic and wild vertigo. The living room drapes pulsing with coloured emergency lights. It takes a few seconds to recognize that these lights are from a snowplow and road salter making their way down the avenue.

I'm suddenly awake and squinting against the daylight coming in through the living room window. Mother is in the kitchen in her bathrobe, somehow having not woken me as she prepared her breakfast. But now there is another mystery. I check the house and Aisha is gone, although her backpack remains in the bedroom. How could she have slipped past and out the door without disturbing me?

When I return to the living room, Mother has her own questions.

"That girl," she begins, "in your bed . . ."

"She's just a friend, Mother. Aisha. She was a neighbour, remember? She lived in unit two with her father. She was smart in school."

"She was the scholarship girl," Mother says, nodding. "What does she do now?"

"I'm not too sure."

"You're not too sure?"

"No. Not really."

"Her jeans are very tight."

"They're not that tight, Mother. Look, her father . . . He died not long ago. And so I invited her to spend some time here."

"To spend time in your bed," she mutters.

"She's here for the *neighbourhood*. To *see* and *remember*."

I know I've raised my voice, but I'm battling my own doubts about the point and wisdom of my invitation. I still don't understand how I could have overslept or why Aisha slipped out from the house, and right now I have other things to do. And so when Mother begins to ask yet again about the woman in her house, I say it in language I don't normally use with her.

"She's here to grieve."

She quiets, pinches her bathrobe around her throat. For a moment, I feel almost ashamed to have pressed the point. But when Mother responds, her voice is polite and sincere.

"The poor thing."

I cannot wait for Aisha to return for I am already late for work. I hurriedly pack up some leftover rice and peas for myself and then walk the ten blocks to the Easy Buy, the big discount food superstore that displaced an old strip mall. I have worked at the Easy Buy for five years, but I know that if I miss a shift, or if I arrive too late, I risk future employment. Business has been good at the store, its aisles crowded with shoppers filling their carts. Shifts are increasingly difficult to get, with many more people willing to work than there are positions available.

The assistant manager, Manny, was raised in the Park not far from my place, although he now lives in what he braggingly calls the "good neighbourhood" of Port Junction. He still has contacts in the Park, though, perhaps family or friends, because he is somehow able to track my daily movements. He knows that I "lurk" around the neighbourhood on walks for no good reason, and that on certain days, if I don't have a shift, I can be found "idling" in the public library. And through this false sense of familiarity with me, he takes it upon himself to lecture me in front of others in the staff room. He lectures me about the risks of associating with the wrong people. He lectures me about people pulling themselves up by their bootstraps and saving money and not expecting handouts. It's about *attitude*. It's about possessing the right *mindset*. The worst is when Manny conducts surprise searches of our lockers for drugs and minor thefts, searches that never result in any finds, and which may or may not be legal in the first place, and which we seem to have no choice but to tolerate. "No worries if you're not doing anything, right?" he explains. Once he found a library copy of *Giovanni's Room* in my locker. He smirked at the photo of the blond man on the cover, and then joked loudly about skids of coconuts and Oreo cookies waiting to be unpacked in the storeroom. "You know," he explained to one of the newer workers, slapping him on the chest, "coloured on the outside, white on the in?"

None of my co-workers, all part-time, and many with families, will dare object or show annoyance. And I have to be careful, too. I do my job, but Manny knows full well that I'm in a bind, being forced because of Mother to find work relatively close to home. Also, despite Manny's warnings about handouts and corruption, he's all too happy to hire under the table those desperate for half the ordinary pay, while he quietly divides the other half with the manager.

And so it's no surprise that today I'm paired with someone new. He's got grey in his hair but muscles and veins like ropes under his skin. When I say hello he nods but doesn't answer. For the next while we begin long hours unloading and itemizing frozen produce and boxed and dried and canned goods from dozens of skids. Sugary cereal and fruit drinks and cookies and chips. The work is endless, repetitive, and my arms begin to give out after three hours. My co-worker looks twice my age or more, but he's strong and he pushes me through the job. At the break, I try speaking to him, but he just nods his head.

We tough it out into the final hour and finish with already stiffening limbs. I'm beside him, taking my coat from my locker, when I try phrases, hopefully not lewd, in what little I've picked up of Tamil and Tagalog.

"Hablas español?" I try next.

"Look, bitch. I'm from Mississauga."

I walk home in the dark. I'm hunched down against the wind and cold, and there is a needled burning in my spine. A passing car splashes me with slush, soaks me right through even worse than last night with Aisha, and my mind turns bitterly to the woman I've invited into my already complicated household. We are struggling, Mother and I, in more ways than one, and we do not need the added weight of more grief, particularly of someone who's not been stuck at home and in a shit job. Someone with options. Someone who's managed to get away.

The rusted squeak of metal grows louder over the wind, and I look up. In the courtyard of a nearby tower is an asphalt lot and a set of swings that have hung since my childhood. There's a child on the swings pumping hard, leaning her body into each swoop up and out, the chain buckling with each fall down. But then I see this is no child but an adult wearing an unbuttoned full-length raincoat and a long and heavy dark skirt, her clothes flapping about her. I walk closer and see her face.

"Aisha?" I call.

She doesn't respond, maybe she doesn't hear. I watch the slick on her forehead. I watch the poles anchoring the swings rocking dangerously upon the sodden earth.

I SPOTTED HER ON THE HOT NIGHT of the shootings, among the other neighbours watching quietly as the cops stood with Francis and me on the doorstep with Mother. She wore her hair bunched to the side of her head in a puffed and off-kilter ponytail, and she was standing with her father, who rested his hand on her shoulder. I risked a careful wave, but she didn't return it. She was watching me, seeing me as if for the first time. And only after I gestured a second time did she respond. With a secret wave, hand close to her body.

The cops were explaining to Mother what had happened and why they had stopped us. There had been an altercation, perhaps a business deal gone bad. Guns were drawn. Two young men were hit but managed to stumble away. There was one fatality, someone known to police, but there were other casualties too, the cops now informed us. Bullets had flown through glass doors and windows. A bystander was shot in his arm. A stray bullet had pierced the thin wall of a unit and struck a sleeping seven-year-old girl.

"A girl," said Mother, as if to herself. "A sleeping child."

Since witnessing Anton get shot, Francis had been a zombie, his eyes glazed and evasive. But Mother's words appeared to shake him awake. For a second he met my eyes, but then dropped his. Mother was now staring at him.

The cops reassured her that we were not under investigation. Already there were leads on the names and whereabouts of the suspects, but since we had been in the vicinity of the shooting, they might want to interview us as the case developed. They voiced concerns about Francis's connections to some of the suspects. Mother nodded and said twice that her boys would cooperate fully. The cops encouraged her, also, to get in touch if she felt she could offer any relevant information. It would all be anonymous, they insisted. Our identities would be protected.

"We *will* cooperate," said Mother again. "We promise. Thank you, officers."

She continued thanking them as they walked away. And then she held the door open for Francis and me to go inside. She shut the door very carefully behind us and took her time letting go of the handle. She seemed to muster all of the energy in her body just to face us.

"You *will* . . . tell me . . . *everything*," she said.

She was looking at Francis, but he didn't meet her eyes. She repeated herself, and then asked Francis if he heard what she had said. He was biting his fingernails down to the quick. He inspected the ragged tip of his smallest finger, squeezed up a little red bead of blood.

"*Francis!*"

He backed up without looking, knocking over a side-table lamp as he rushed to our bedroom. Mother and I followed and stood in the doorway as he went to work. He grabbed his busted white-and-red Adidas bag and moved about the room stuffing into it whatever was easily at hand.

"What are you doing?" asked Mother.

He didn't answer, just kept adding to his bag essential things like underwear and socks but also weird choices, like the reindeer-patterned sleeveless sweater that he'd refused to wear at least a decade ago. When he pulled a hoody from one of his drawers and tried to shove it into his bag, Mother gripped its sleeve.

"Where are you going?"

"Nowhere," he said.

"I have *asked* you a question. Where?"

"Nowhere. Please let go."

"You *will* tell me where you're going."

"Please let me go. Please."

There was a brief struggle as Mother tried to pull the hoody away from him, and when Francis used his strength and weight to tug it from her grasp, she stumbled forward and struck her head hard on the bunk bed. There was silence and stillness as she looked at her eldest son, her hand on her forehead, her eyes wide and blinking.

For the first time since shots were fired that night, Francis wore an expression of pain on his wet face. Mother checked her hand for blood but found none. Francis said sorry. *Sorry.* And then he fled the room with his hoody and bag. The sound of the front door opening but not shutting, the tinkling of the security chain.

Mother and I waited up all night for Francis to come back. By three in the morning, she had moved to her bed, lying there in her stained uniform, her shoes still on, a small egg of a bruise on her forehead, purple ugly, which she wouldn't allow me to tend. I put on the table beside her a glass of water, as well as some crackers and slices of banana, but she didn't take a bite. I brought in the fan from the living room. She didn't respond, she didn't move or even seem to blink.

"Just rest," I told her. "I'll worry about Francis."

She pressed her eyes tightly closed at the mention of his name, and then I did as I promised I would do, I worried about Francis. I thought as hard as I could about his new friends. I thought especially about a skinny kid named Jelly, who I knew lived in the same building as Anton and had become Francis's closest friend. I knew that Jelly had been stopped by police, but so had many. I wondered where Francis might have gone, where he would have looked for safety.

A boy named Jelly. A barbershop called Desirea's.

When the sky began to fill with a heavy orange light, you could tell that the heat was going to be just as oppressive as the day before. Mother went to the bathroom and then appeared in the kitchen wearing fresh work clothes. She sat at the kitchen table to eat her porridge, but when she tried to stand, she suddenly sat back down. I stared at her. She blinked, looked at me accusingly, and then stood.

"I'm fine," she said.

"I'm walking you to the stop."

Cop cars and news vans still crowded our block. A small group of neighbours crammed into the slanted shade cast by the bus shelter. Women in cleaning uniforms, men in thick jeans and safety boots, everyone's clothes already darkening with sweat around necks and underarms. These might have been the same people who had watched Francis and me brought home by the cops the night before, but I couldn't tell. No one was willing to meet our eyes.

A full bus drove by, unable to pick up a single passenger. The temperature was rising by the minute, and though everyone was still quiet, there was an impatient shifting of feet, and a few glances our way.

"Thug youths," one woman said. "Predators. *Criminals*." She pronounced "cri-mi-*nals*" the way Mother did. Nobody waiting for the bus even looked up. It was too hot to respond or to acknowledge such talk, which had not been directed at anyone in particular.

"Their parents," she said. "Above all, their *parents*."

Mother's face seemed ready to break. It's hard to describe. Like watching a glass ball being dropped in a slow-motion movie. That fraction of a second just after the glass hits the ground and it's still a ball, but the cracks are everywhere, and you know it's not going to be a ball much longer.

It took another ten minutes for the next bus to arrive, and, climbing on, Mother paused, gripping the bars, before recovering. The bus headed off, the cooked-up fumes of diesel and hot asphalt as it went. The shimmer of the street and the world all around, a deep-gut sickness, dizziness. I managed to avoid falling, sliding down the glass side of the shelter to the sidewalk.

———

Until that moment, my relationship with Aisha appeared to be based upon the most fragile and quiet of connections. I had certainly never before considered knocking on her door, and I knew that on that scorched morning after the chaos of the shootings I had chosen the very worst time to do so. I walked around to her unit and rapped twice on her door. The yellow light in the peephole flickered as someone peered out at me, and then locks were undone, the safety chain unhitched, and the door opened by the very person I'd hoped not to see.

Aisha's father wasn't the only single father in the Park, but he was one of the most distinctive. Samuel was small and slim and quiet and very dark. He came from the same rural district in Trinidad as our mother. And it was rumoured that he had been a teacher there. But here, he worked as a security guard, his uniform always at least three sizes too big for him, his loose pants rustling in the wind. He moved "loitering" kids along from seats and doorways at malls and fast-food joints, and he'd had an encounter or two with Francis and me, but these weren't at all on my mind as he stood before me on that sweltering morning, staring with all the uncertainty you'd expect after seeing me brought home by the cops the night before.

"Yes?" he asked tightly. "May I help you?"

Aisha rescued me by calling out, "It's all right, Dad," and then quickly appearing behind her father, stamping on some sandals. Her hair was wet, and she was wearing shorts and a tank top that showed her back and shoulders. I felt a foolish stab of desire as I watched the subtle negotiation play itself out between daughter and father, some hushed but intense exchange of words, and then a sharp look of warning from Aisha that seemed to make the man back down. Samuel tried cupping his hand on her shoulder as a final bit of persuasion, but she shrugged it off and pushed out the door and past me towards the sidewalk.

"The library," she said.

We walked a dozen blocks to the green-glassed building. Stepping into it, I felt the sharpness of the air conditioning, felt the wet skin of my shirt clinging. Whenever we visited the library together, we would always try to get seats at a table beside a green-tinted window. And although the library was busy that day, we managed to score it, the plastic sticky beneath our bare legs. Around us were ordinary people from the Park. Mothers with restless young children, a young man frowning down at what looked to be a textbook, older men in their mismatched combinations of suit jackets and baseball caps, some reading newspapers in different languages. One held a paper with a headline story about the shooting the night before. Aisha grabbed a paperback from a swivel rack and riveted her eyes upon the pages, flipping randomly.

I spoke to her in a whisper. "Did you hear the cops

caught the suspects? There were five. Most weren't even from the Park. Anyway, I think it's all over now. I think everyone's safe."

She kept flipping pages, her anger seething. In her haste, she had chosen one of those after-school-special books for teenaged girls, something I knew she hated.

"Aisha . . . ?" I asked.

"It was Goose," she said.

Her voice was sharp, and she had to give herself a moment before telling me what she had heard. Goose had been asleep in her bedroom when the shooting started, and after being hit by a bullet she dragged herself to her closet. She lost consciousness, unable to answer while her mother called and ran wildly through the house looking for her. A paramedic joining the search noticed the creep of red staining the carpet just outside the closet.

"They say she's stable now," Aisha said. "They're calling her lucky."

I knew Goose only a little. I didn't know how she got her nickname, but I knew she rode a bike with purple streamers on the handlebars. I remember Francis once helped her put her bike chain back on because Goose didn't want to get her hands "gweesy."

"Aisha," I said, "I know you saw the cops bring me and Francis home. I still don't know everything. But me and Francis . . . You *know* us, right?"

She held my eyes for the first time that morning. She nodded, went back to reading, and I felt the first small relief in hours.

Aisha and I had been neighbours most of our lives, but for the years of childhood and the first years of high school we never really spoke. We were roughly the same age, but she had skipped grades and then entered a special enrichment program, which I imagined to be full of goofs all sloppy-mouthed with braces and classroom answers. As a child, mosquito-thin, she biked around haphazardly and wore asymmetrical ponytails. As a teenager, she wore tights and sweaters that revealed a bra strap and the brown points of her shoulders. Two months before we began something like a friendship, during her last semester of high school, I watched her receive a special achievement award for math and science during a school assembly. She had won an entrance scholarship to a university in Montreal and, according to the principal, would be going away by the end of the summer. She was the sort of girl the world considers "an example" or "the exception," the sort of girl my mother described as having "a future." She stood onstage in the auditorium, posing with a frozen smile for the photograph, and, somehow, she caught me looking at her from the crowd.

A month later, in July, I spotted her sitting behind the green-tinted glass of the public library. She was wearing shorts and reading a large book with a slight frown on her face. Dust motes hung lazily in the air, and her eyelashes were touched blue by the sunlight pouring down. There was a strange play of image and light on the glass. I watched my own reflection mingle with the sight of her reading. A many-limbed monster. And then something alarming happened: she saw me and smiled.

Francis had never been one to offer truths about girls or desire or the riddles of sex. Instead, he had usually seemed almost as confused as I was. Once, when we were both very young and sneaking peeks into a ground-level apartment of a neighbouring building, we saw a couple hunched naked into each other while, in the background, a television played the game show *Definition*. We watched their urgent struggling, the woman's face out of view, the man's face purple-bloated with effort. And at the end of their exercise, we caught what might have been one of the most haunting mysteries of childhood: the man's face contorted not with pleasure but with pain.

"An *orgasm*," Francis had whispered to me, once we had fled far from the scene. The glistening horror of that word.

A couple years later, Francis and I were approached by a man who lived far to the east of our home, in the "good" neighbourhood of Port Junction. He was arranging a showing of a porno film, an actual film in black and white projected on to a basement wall of his bungalow. For a dollar, we found ourselves on a couch in that darkened damp space with the man and eight other boys, all older than us. We sat together in the stink of their collective fear and excitement, our bare legs against each other, and I appeared to be the only one to notice our host discreetly pulling himself and only occasionally watching the images. Either the film had no volume or else the man had turned the sound off, and the quiet charged the brutal acts of the grey-white bodies on the wall with the same strange aura of meaningfulness and authority as old-fashioned silent movies.

Francis never gave me "the talk." He provided no tips or warnings. He offered none of that information, urgently shared by many young men we knew, about the various "types" of girls and what they each would "do." And this was all the more puzzling and sometimes disappointing because Francis, unlike most boys, who simply talked shit, had actually received real and positive attention. When he passed a group of girls on the street, they'd pull themselves close to whisper then laugh approvingly. Even the silent daughter at the convenience store counter would give him a sly smile when handing him change, her eyes on his ass as he walked away. But when I pressed him for stories of the wild encounters he was rumoured to have enjoyed ("Francis, *dog*," some neighbourhood boys would shout out to him), he just shook his head. And once, when I cornered him about the three condoms I had seen in his bedroom drawer under his socks, he shouted at me for getting into his stuff, and then, knowing that an explanation was needed, he mumbled something about "fucking bitches" in a voice so obviously put on that it did nothing but humiliate us both.

I'd had no real experiences of my own. And so, on that day in July, just a month before the shootings, when Aisha suddenly met my eyes through the glass of the library, I felt a sudden vulnerability. I pulled the chill metal handles of the glass doors and then jammed my hands deep into my pockets, my head down with the brim of my cap pulled over my eyes. I steeled myself when passing through those book detectors at the entrance, imagining that an alarm would sound, that everyone would see me trying to stroll in like it was nothing. There was no alarm, there were no snickers at the sight of me in this space, and I managed to vanish into one of the aisles of books.

I decided that I needed ammunition. I pulled from a display marked "Classics" a paperback copy of *The Theban Plays*, which showed on its cover a white mask with hollow eyes bleeding red, the mouth set open in an expression of terrible sorrow. Armed, I walked to the table where Aisha was sitting.

"Hey," I said. "Can . . . *May* I sit?"

A group of neighbourhood kids seated nearby leaned their heads in together to giggle. Aisha shoved her pile of books and magazines aside to make room for me beside her. I noticed that the "example" of a girl wasn't reading anything educational at all, but instead *People* magazine. I didn't look at Aisha, but immediately opened my "classic" and studiously fixed my eyes on the page, the words swimming there unreadable. After long minutes, I nodded as if I had absorbed some timeless truth. I could feel Aisha looking at me, sense the growing ridiculousness of the situation, but I wouldn't lift my attention from the page, wouldn't abandon my performance. Until Aisha said it softly.

"Hey in there."

Our relationship started this way, and the weather helped. As the heat intensified that summer, we took shelter in the air-conditioned cool of the library. For a short while, I continued choosing books I thought might impress her, mostly Penguin Classics, but once a book of anatomy. (Those unskinned bodies, that heart diagrammed all red and blue and ugly.) But Aisha was interested that summer only in trashy entertainment and music magazines. She'd touch my arm to read aloud some gossip about LL Cool J, guffawing in a way that drew stern looks from the small community of readers in the library. Her chair drawn closer to show me another bit of celebrity gossip, her bare calf lightly touching mine.

She was, I began to think, maybe just a bit like me, another black mongrel, her hair and eyes in part from a Filipina mother who, for some reason, had to leave the country. But, really, Aisha was only herself. That chicken pox scar on her nose. Or that tiny dot with a tail at the edge of her pupil, a tadpole near a whirlpool of black.

"I have to go," Aisha now told me, looking up at the library's clock.

"I'll walk with you," I said.

It was getting close to eleven in the morning, and the margin of shade cast by the buildings had shrunk to almost nothing. In the courtyard of a neighbouring building, someone had set out a turtle-shaped swimming pool for the kids. One little girl carefully dipping her foot into the water that had probably already turned to soup. Before we made our way back to the Waldorf, we stopped off at a convenience store, and Aisha bought a can of Sprite. We shared it while sitting on the curb of the old parking lot near our units. There was a boy thumping a basketball on the sticky asphalt. An empty cop car was parked on the side of the lot. Another cop car was visible a block away. And then still another car drifted slowly past us on the avenue, pulled to a stop a block ahead.

"Really?" Aisha said. "Three?"

I shrugged, and she took another sip from the can. Nearby on the shaded concrete curb was a mother gently rocking her baby, and both had their eyes closed. They had probably been up all night. Aisha touched my arm to hand me her Sprite, and I noticed on the lip of the can the pearl of liquid that had touched her mouth. I sipped, and handed the rest back to her. She drained the can and stood to go home, but before she did she gave me a hug goodbye. I felt the slick on her arms as she lifted them over my shoulder, I felt her stomach and for the first time her hips pressed against me. There was a long pause, a moment in which all sorts of things suddenly became possible, but then a siren wailed, and just as suddenly all was lost.

A cop car pulled up beside a group of young men who had been walking down the sidewalk. The siren was quickly cut, but it triggered every one of us. The baby woke and started crying. The mother's eyes snapped open, and when she recognized me, she stared as if I were a stray and possibly rabid dog. The fragile peace was broken, nerves flayed once again, but could this really explain what Aisha did next? She looked down and spotted a broken chunk of asphalt that she loosened further with the heel of her sneaker. She picked it up, stepped back for balance, and hurled. It hit a window of the empty police car, making a sharp sound like the breaking of hard candy in your mouth, spider-webbing the glass into a pattern of pale blue without breaking.

A cold hard panic in my bowels, my head and chest pounding. The cops far down the street didn't seem to hear or notice, and they just continued questioning the youths. I looked at Aisha, this girl I thought I'd known or at least glimpsed, brushing from her damp face a strand of curly hair, setting her eyes hard at me, daring me to say something.

How could I? Of all the things that had happened after the shooting, this was by far the craziest.

THREE

She's become a writer, she tells us, the paid kind. After fleeing the Park a decade ago, she dove into a general science degree, before declaring in her second year a major in computer science. She attacked coding languages and algorithms and data structures with a single-mindedness that unsettled everyone around her. "Do you ever relax?" asked a classmate, and the room laughed. "*Do* you ever relax?" asked her lab supervisor, one evening, when they were alone. She steeled herself, avoided all company, graduated with the second-highest average of her class, but didn't, unlike most others, immediately land a full-time job. Was she unconsciously cold in interviews? Was that it? She did, eventually, begin working as a programmer in a large and successful IT start-up. She spent two years in a room of mostly young men, bracing herself against the monitor stink, the perspiration, the banter, until she finally went rogue. She's now a "hired gun," she explains, a freelance programmer for short-term projects, mostly GIS-related, and never more than a few weeks. In the past three months, she's worked in both Manila and Austin. Before that, she says, she helped design and implement a cable network solution in the capital of Uganda.

"Kampala," says Mother.

Aisha smiles and lifts her cup of tea to Mother before sipping. We are sitting in the living room washed in morning light, on this third day of Aisha's visit. Spring is finally beginning to show. Through the living room window, we can see an old woman setting out small flowerpots and planters on her doorstep, a man hanging wet clothes on a balcony clothesline. On the sidewalk, a bunch of kids are playing basketball beside the thawing of grey snow. Aisha takes a bite of her buttered sweetbread, and she speaks again in a lowered tone.

"A year ago, after a stint in Venezuela, I caught a flight on my own coin to Trinidad. I visited the village where my father was born. Where you were born too, Ruth. I saw the cane fields now wild. I saw the white church of the Spiritual Baptists. You remember it all, don't you, Ruth? I've been thinking a lot about that place since my father died."

The wet smack of a basketball outside. Mother nods, takes another sip of her tea, swallows slowly.

"Tell me about Kampala," she says.

For the rest of the morning, Aisha sits with Mother chatting quietly about the many places she has visited, but never returning to the matter of their personal losses. Neither appears at all interested in including me, and sometimes they seem outright secretive. In the early afternoon, I walk in on them whispering together on the couch. I catch a burst of shared laughter, the first time I've heard Mother laugh in a while.

"I've been wondering," Aisha tells me later that night when Mother is asleep. "Could I plan a get-together? Just a gathering, really, with food and music, maybe a few words spoken about the people we've lost, Francis especially."

She reads my face but continues explaining. "It doesn't have to be elaborate. It really doesn't have to be formal in any way. It could be as simple as a dinner. We'd invite a few of the boys from Francis's life."

"Most have moved away," I say. "Others . . . It's been ten years, people just want to move on."

"It won't hurt to ask them. They can always say no. Also, others might want to come. Younger people. Kids dealing with their own stuff today."

"I don't think so, Aisha. My mother doesn't need a group of strangers in her home."

"They wouldn't be strangers. They'd be people I've met. Kids from neighbourhoods like ours. Some international students from the city campuses. Just people trying to make sense of things."

"Let them make sense of things somewhere else. I'm sorry, Aisha, I can't allow this right now. It won't work."

"This would be good for your mother. This would be good for you, too."

"Don't tell me what's good for us, Aisha."

"You know she's not well, right, Michael? The way she drifts. The way she wanders. Yesterday, when you were at work, we were talking about the old neighbours, and she excused herself to start searching for something she couldn't describe to me. She ended up wandering outside, still searching. I watched her cross the avenue without even looking. I had to shout for her to turn and wait."

"She's getting older . . ."

"It's got absolutely nothing to do with age. You know that. Your mother's like this because she's still mourning. Or else she's unable to mourn. It's been ten years and she still can't accept. She's stuck."

I know that Aisha is talking about "complicated grief." I've heard the term used by doctors, and I've read books from the library. There are losses that mire a person in mourning, that prevent them from moving forward by making sense of the past. You become disoriented, assailed by loops of memory, by waking dreams and hallucinations. I don't need any of this explained to me, but I'm reminded by Aisha's face that she's grieving too. I breathe out, nod in a noncommittal way.

"Let me think about it," I offer. "She's been doing all right lately. I just don't want to complicate things for her."

The following day, it happens. Aisha and I go for a short early-morning walk, and we return to an empty house. I reassure Aisha, but within ten minutes there's a shy knock at the door, and when I answer it, it's a neighbourhood boy, Sivi.

"Your mother," he says, "she's in the valley. She's not wearing shoes."

I avoid looking at Aisha while slipping quickly back into my coat and shoes. We walk down the avenue to the edge of the bridge. We step over the guardrail and spend time rummaging around until we find the entrance to the rabbit path, hidden among young trees and withered brush and cluttered papers and plastic. We push forward and down through the scrub and low branches and slippery matted gunk of leaves. Soon the sounds of traffic have softened until we're submerged from the city and walking a quiet paved path through the skeletons of trees, their branches bare and dark and wet.

"I know where she is," I tell Aisha.

Just beyond the path, through the underbrush, there's a clearing beside the creek. The water is higher and faster than usual because of the spring runoff. And here Mother is standing about ten feet away from the edge. There's no need to approach her right away, no need to rush, and I stay with Aisha at a distance. The sunlight is brittle but bright. The water in the creek is tinged brown and olive, and it makes a nice rushing noise over the smooth grey stones. Tendrils of moss blow under the water. There are some small flowers already beginning to bloom at the water's edge, very light blue, very small. Mother moves towards them now, lifting her skirt to get through the thistles, and eventually standing right at the creek's edge. She reaches down to the nearest petals, cupping them tenderly in her hands.

Here, the pillars of the bridge are covered with graffiti tags and drawings, faces of people like those in the Park, and higher up, in the wedge of shelter just beneath the street level, there's a stained mattress and evidence of a fire and crushed cans of food and beer. Aisha is quiet. And when I look there are flashes of light upon her arms, sun speckling through the moving trees. Coins of light on her face.

"She gets into states," I say, quietly. "It's not all the time."

Mother has noticed us now. She turns and adjusts the collar of her winter coat. The bottom of her skirt is stained damp, and she tries to hide from our sight her bare feet, her toes blackened with mud. She has a small bunch of the blue flowers in her hand, a bright blue, an unnameable pretty colour. Singular.

TWO DAYS AFTER FRANCIS LEFT HOME, I woke late, my clothes soaked with sweat. I rose dizzily to my feet, squinting hard against the light, and I began to search the kitchen. For some time, Francis had been bringing home milk and juice at least, occasionally fruit, and once in a while chicken or fish. But now that he was gone, the cupboards were empty. The last bit of butter had been forgotten out in the sun, filling its dish with bright yellow for the ants. I checked the fridge: a quarter carton of milk gone bad, the machine powerless against the heat. The only real food was a Tupperware container of rice and peas that looked too old to eat. An empty juice jug, a bottle of pepper sauce. A jar of baby dill pickles. I fished one out with my fingers to crunch.

The early-afternoon sun had swung around the building and was now flooding thick into the living room. I carefully closed the drapes and drank water mixed with spoons of sugar for taste and it ran out of my skin like I was some spaghetti sieve. I tried watching game shows, but it was too hot. I tried soaking my head in the bathroom sink filled with cold water. I tried adjusting the drapes, and looking through the glass, I noticed the windows of some of the apartments facing us, and I saw what seemed to be a solution. I fetched tinfoil from the kitchen and I taped sheets of it to the windows, slowly smoothing out the metal crinkles with the palm of my hand.

Glide of my sweat on the foil.

I was watching cartoons when Mother came back from work. She looked wrecked. She looked into the fridge. She held the pickle bottle up to the unusually weak light, observing the spices swirling in the liquid, her brow raised as though she were making a calculation.

"Is this it?" she asked.

"Is this what?"

"Is this all you plan on eating today?"

"I'm not really hungry."

She looked about the darkened room. Then she saw it, saw what I had done to the windows.

"What is that?" she asked.

"It's tinfoil."

"I can see it's tinfoil. What's it doing there?"

"I put it up to reflect the sun."

Cartoon classical music sounded from the television as Mother stared at me.

"Is that what I look like to you?" she said, her voice edgy, halting. She gestured again to the window. "Like the sort of woman who puts tinfoil up on she windows? Like the sort of woman who advertises 'tinfoil' to everyone passing on the street?"

"It's not a bad idea. I mean, other people do it."

"And am I other people?" she said, the volume building in her voice. "Do you stand there and look at your mother, your *own* mother, and think, *look*! There she is! My mother! *Other people*!"

I didn't know how to respond. I didn't think it'd be a good idea to try. When I looked over at her, she hadn't moved. She was still holding the pickle jar. More music from the television, the cwazy wabbit fleeing, legs blurring.

A jar exploded against the wall behind me and sent shards flying all over the place. Then quiet. Something wet was on my upper lip, and I touched it carefully with my tongue, fearing blood. Mother righted herself after the effort of her throw, looked behind me to the wall, to the glazed pattern on the wall, the broken glass on the floor.

"Are you cut?" she asked.

"I'm okay."

"You're touching your face."

"It's just pickle juice."

The fridge door was still open, and she slumped against the handle, her chin pressed strangely into her neck. She stayed like that for a moment, and then she breathed out and blinked as if she'd just woken up. She looked deep into the fridge, used her fingernail to scratch at some stain on the vegetable crisper. Shook her head, the sheen of light upon her face.

"Do you smell that?" she asked. "The dill?"

In the library that evening, Aisha told me that Goose had been moved out of intensive care. She was doing much better. Word had gone out that she had a rare blood type, and donors had volunteered from around the city. Aisha went silent. She was studying what looked like an algebra textbook. More than studying—staring down the equations. I decided not to mention the asphalt she'd thrown at the window of the cop car. Instead I sat quietly for a good length of time, combing through the newspaper coverage of the shooting.

There were updates, columns, letters to the editor. A lot of people were angry about the way Goose had suffered. Some called for a crackdown on crime, others for much more. One columnist wrote in that old and ready-made language about "immigrants" and "ethnic neighbourhoods" and "sending people back where they came from," even though most in the Park knew that the suspects had all been raised in the surrounding city. But what caught my attention in one story was a photo of Anton, identified as both known to police and deceased. It was one of those high school photos that for so many of us always seem to go wrong. The photographer didn't choose the right background or adjust the light settings, and so the outlines of Anton's face and hair bled into the navy behind him. His eyes steeled, his mouth screwed tight upon his face.

What did I know about Anton, this boy whom few would mourn? He lived in the Park, in a sagging low-rise complex on a muddy lot. He shared a two-bedroom unit with his parents, his two brothers, and three sisters, all elbowing for room in a place barely as big as anyone else's living room. Most times he seemed to live bare and in the open. He never had the right sort of clothes against the cold and rain. He couldn't hide the fact that at dinnertime he wouldn't be going inside, or that he'd never visited a dentist. At all hours, he could be seen hanging out on the bench in the courtyard of my building, calling out jokey violent threats to me whenever I passed by.

I had no reason whatsoever to like Anton. But once, I saw his world close in hard upon him. A pack of men from outside the neighbourhood hunted him down and caught him in a field not far from the Park where there was just enough darkness for the work to be done. They roughed him up, made him bleed from his nose and mouth, kicked his legs and stomach over and over again with their boots. I caught the last bit of this from a distance, but was probably alone in doing so since there was very little noise. Anton never called out for help. The attackers finished their business by pulling off much of his clothing and leaving him half-naked.

I approached carefully, and when I got close enough, I heard Anton crying. He had his hands over his eyes, a wheezy sound in his throat, crumpled face, and tears that were hard to distinguish from the muddy filth he'd been left in. When he saw me, he turned his face away, but then he started pretending that he'd been laughing, his sobs turning to chuckles, the laughter becoming almost real. I watched with mixed feelings of concern and annoyance, until I finally asked what the hell was so funny. Anton shook his head, trying to catch his breath and voice from the waves of laughter now shaking him. He couldn't tell, wouldn't explain. It was a joke, he said, a dirty joke. Way too dirty for a little bitch like me, he said.

"You seen Francis yet?" Aisha asked, startling me back to the library.

"Not yet," I answered.

"How's your mother?" she asked next.

"She's, you know, okay."

She nodded and went back to reading. I hadn't planned to tell her about Mother's outburst, but a few minutes later, when the overhead lights of the library flashed to warn us of closing time, I changed my mind. As we rose to go, I mentioned the pickle-throwing incident as casually as possible.

"You need to tell Francis," Aisha told me.

"He's probably with his friends at Desirea's."

"So? Go visit him."

"I've never been there before. He hasn't invited me."

"He's your brother. What sort of invitation do you need?"

I walked alone down the avenue and towards the intersection of Markham and Lawrence. During the day, the whole area bustled, but now, just after sunset, even the convenience stores were closed, their windows dark and empty looking. Despite its bright, unshielded security lights, the parking lot facing the avenue seemed haunted.

A cop car passed by. Its flashers on, but no siren.

Desirea's was at the back of the mall, in the much less desirable wing. The area here wasn't as well lit. The windows of the cheaper storefronts were cracked or boarded up. I passed a rusted orange dumpster bleeding a sludgy

75

smear towards a storm sewer. There were pools of oily standing water and the funk of garbage.

One business looked open. Thumping music edging on noise coming from within. There was no sign advertising services provided or wares sold, no spiralling pole set out front. The windows papered with posters for concerts and dances and parties, a clutter of print that seemed designed to obstruct rather than to inform.

"Shut the door, fool!" a voice shouted at me. "The air conditioning."

Entering Desirea's, you walked into a solid fog of smell, a collision of body warmth, colognes and hair products, thick in the nose, waxy on the tongue. You were hit with a mash-up of sounds and rhythms halted and restarted. A bass so deep and heavy you could feel it in your jaw.

"Yo, Dru," said a voice. "Tell this punk we're booked solid till midnight."

A dozen young men sat on cracked vinyl couches or beat-up chairs. They were wearing loose jeans and stencilled shirts; baseball caps with flat rims cocked sideways; hair picked out or slicked back; do-rags or fades with sharp and sorcerous cuts. I recognized Dru, the thick man who ran the shop. He was standing at a barber's chair, cutting the hair of a young man who now lowered his folded newspaper to stare at me. That picture of Anton again. Dru now gesturing at me with his clippers, yelling over the music.

"Hear that, little man? We got no walk-ins this evening."

"Guy needs attention, Dru. Check out the car-wreck hair!"

"Hold up, should someone get Francis? Isn't that his brother?"

Just then, the music changed, and I caught the set-up of turntables in the corner. Standing there, surrounded by yellow milk crates of albums, his attention fully on the record spinning before him, was Francis's friend Jelly, but in a state I'd never seen before, never imagined. Still minding the turntables, he pulled a record from a crate, cued it up, flicked switches, held a headphone to his ear with a cocked shoulder. The backbeats changed, and then a high, pained voice filled the room, maybe a woman's, maybe a man's, slowed under the friction of his hand, human but barely so. Mourning against the almost deafening rhythm.

When Francis appeared, he took me to a room in the back of the shop. A bedsheet covered the small window, and I could see, besides cleaning supplies and bike parts and a broken barber's chair and more milk crates of records, some of his clothes hung up to dry as well as the cot that he must be using as a bed. His face was screwed up bad at me. I'd showed up unannounced, but when I told him about the tinfoil, the pickle jar, Mother's state, his expression softened. He said he'd give me some money for groceries and asked if I'd had anything to eat that day. I shook my head.

"Okay," he said. "Just give me a second."

He went back to Jelly, and as they talked I got my first real look at Francis's friend. He was thin and dark, with a patch of onion brown on his temple shaped, somehow, like a forgotten continent. They were whispering, their heads bent into each other. Jelly passed my brother a set of keys, and they slipped palms and joined fingers and hugged and stayed, and when they pulled apart there were sweat marks where their bodies had touched. Jelly spotted me watching them, and he chinned a greeting.

"Come on," Francis told me. "Let's get going."

We left the shop and he walked me towards an old Honda convertible with the top left down. Hub caps were missing, and paint was stripped from a good third of its outside. Francis got in and started the car, doing all this very carefully and deliberately. I hesitated, then opened the passenger door and settled in. I started doing up the seat belt but then, catching Francis's frown, let go of it. Francis turned the ignition key once more even though the engine was already running, and this made the most frightening pterodactyl sound I've ever heard. He told me to stop jinxing him by looking so worried, and he concentrated once more and then shifted the car into first gear and touched a pedal. A sharp burning smell came up, and he took the hand brake off before trying the pedal again.

"Whose is this?"

"Mine with Jelly," he said.

"You bought it?"

"Of course we bought it. How else could we get it?"

"When did you learn how to drive?" I asked.

"Quiet! Stop distracting me!"

"Do you have a licence?"

"Yes, I have a licence. Shut the hell up!"

After a lot of reversing and forwarding, we pulled out from the parking lot. We drove through the back alley of the strip mall and, after bumping over the curb, we were off on the avenue, my brother's arm perched showily on the top of the door. He skidded to a fast stop at a traffic light, and once, when he signalled to a guy he knew on the sidewalk, the car veered dangerously, the horn of an oncoming car blasting at us.

"Headlights?" I asked softly.

"I'll find them later."

We went to a grocery store and bought several cans of beans and tuna, as well as rice, condensed milk, and a bag of apples. We put these in the trunk, but instead of going home, Francis kept driving west until he hooked off Lawrence and into the parking lot of the Steak Queen restaurant. A slight rain had started, and this pressed Francis to park more quickly than he should have. In and out of the spot we went until he cut the engine, the car still more than a bit crooked, and with little etches on the bumper of the neighbouring car that we hoped nobody would notice.

In the restaurant, Francis ordered us a feast. Two steaks on buns *and* two burgers as well as fries and onion rings, two deluxe milkshakes made extravagant with whipped cream and cherries and extra syrup. He insisted that we get full-sized salads with Italian dressing "for the vitamins." The man at the cash register seemed doubtful about the order and the look of the two of us until Francis put his money on the counter. It was all in small bills and change, but he even had enough for a tip.

We took a seat while the food was being prepared. An old man sat by himself with only a paper cup before him on the table. A couple tables away from us, three older girls I recognized from the neighbourhood were sharing a sundae. They had done-up nails and hair brightly streaked and they were each almost frighteningly hot when they set their eyes at you. They were looking at Francis, who nodded politely but drummed his hands nervously on the table.

We feasted quietly until we had nothing but fries. We dipped them in ketchup and just nibbled at the ends. I watched the man behind the counter who worked the grill. He was sitting now on a stool with his arms folded on his body, his eyes closed. It was difficult not to feel something for him sitting there, catching snatches of sleep, other times growing old in the squinting smoke while the orders were shouted at him.

"Your friend, Jelly," I began. "He's a DJ or something? He seems pretty cool, even with that nickname. What's with it, anyway?"

Francis shook his head. "You know," he said, "you've got to work on things."

"What do you mean? What things?"

"Like all sorts of things. Like stepping into Desirea's the way you did. Like always looking so unsure. You've got to be cooler about things, and not put everything out on your face all the time. You've got to carry yourself better and think about your look. Doesn't matter how poor you are. You can always turn up the edge of a collar to style a bit, little things like that. You can always do things to let the world know you're not nobody. You never know when your break is coming."

We sat in silence then. I caught Francis looking at me in the window's reflection, but then he looked away. A car passed by on the road with its sound system on full blast, its undercarriage tricked up with light, a purple ghost beneath it on the asphalt.

"I'm taking you to see Dad," he said, very softly, as if to himself, the words seeming to hang in the air between us.

———

Our dad was that man in a badly focused photograph, little more. Mother was reluctant to speak about him, and even as kids we understood that there are things about the past that you just don't press. But she would tell Francis about our father's struggles when he first came to this country. Going to school during the day and washing dishes at night was not easy. Some people wouldn't rent their places to people like him. Some people wouldn't hire men like him, or fairly pay or promote them. There were countless indignities a man *like him* had to face, and there had been tolls, she explained. There had been tolls. She wasn't always this understanding. Once, when Francis asked what our father had studied at school, the reaction was sharp, and she used language we'd never heard in the home. "He *was* studying to be a man," she explained, "but then the bitch dropped out."

But Francis and I understood that we had a special opportunity in our father, greater room for guesswork and imagination than most kids had. Our father could be anything. And from an early age, Francis had developed his own theory. Our father, he announced to me one day, was "a composer."

I wondered why a composer, why not someone who sang or played an instrument. But I never pressed. Even as kids, we had learned to be gentle with each other's hopes and dreams.

"We don't know our dad," I said.

"We don't have to know him. He's our father."

"We don't know *anything* about him. Even where he lives."

"I found out. He's here in Scarborough."

"How did you find that out?"

"I've been asking people."

"For how long? Why didn't you tell me?"

"I'm telling you now."

"Where in Scarborough?"

"He lives in a low-rise called the Oberlin. It's north of the highway."

"That's too far away," I said.

"We've got wheels now, remember?"

"We can't just show up. It's been a long time. It's been . . . forever."

"See?" he said. "That's exactly what I'm talking about. Not trying stuff, not believing. I'm not saying he's going to solve everything for us. I'm not stupid. I'm just saying we'll have a talk. Why not give it a shot?"

The drizzle had turned to rain. The wet black of the street reflected the street lights, and our car and the others hissed loudly. After a few blocks, the rain grew cold and stinging on our faces, and I asked Francis to put the top up, but he didn't know how. Fiddling around, he managed to turn on the wipers, but he also ran a red light, another car skidding to a stop to avoid hitting us.

"Okay," he admitted. "That was close."

"This is crazy," I said. "We need to go home."

"Would you relax? You're completely freaking me out."

The rain drowned out other sounds, and at times we could see almost nothing ahead of us. We were both getting soaked, but Francis just kept driving and looking around, guided by some unseen map.

I have one flickering memory of our father, and of music and dance. I was very young, and I think it was winter, because I remember a cold white light falling in from a window. I remember being shown a record player, the black disc spinning, and a dark hand setting the needle very gently on a clear groove. The beginning of the very best song, a happy song, full of brassy horns. Our parents were dancing to this music in a way at once jokey and joyful, spinning each other around with hooked elbows, threatening to knock over tables and chairs, Francis's thin arms reaching high up towards them.

I remembered him being lifted up and spun. I remembered being spun too. A wheeling room of yellow peeling wallpaper, and a glimpse, and then another, and then another, of my brother's face. Half glee, half alarm. His feet tippy-toed, his arms reaching up.

"My turn," he cried, again and again.

When I got older, I wondered if I really could have remembered this scene. I would have been just a bit more than a year old. How could I remember the peeled wallpaper but not remember Dad's face? Why the dancing, when I'd never, ever, for years after, seen Mother do that?

The pelting of the rain eased up, and we could see more clearly now. We crawled slowly through streets that looked to my eyes all the same.

"There," Francis said. "That's the street. It should be just down here."

He stopped in front a low-rise with a sign saying The Oberlin, and Rooms Not Available. The building was rough, sheets on the windows instead of curtains.

"I want to go home," I said.

"Come on," Francis laughed. "Aren't you curious?"

We stepped from the car and walked wet and ridiculous towards the lobby. Francis held the door open for me, and I paused for a second, frozen at the sight of a big guy inside, maybe driven inside by the rain. Francis pushed me in and, screwing his face up tough and serious, stepped in behind me.

"Sup," he said to the guy, who answered with a flash of gold teeth.

Francis squinted at the buzzer panel. Letters were missing from the names. Cha . . . Fur . . . dan . . . Ho . . . Most of them weren't even half-complete, but Francis searched the scraps of letters, mouthing them aloud, and then punched in a number.

"Yes?" said a woman's voice over the intercom.

"Sorry," said Francis, and he tried another number.

"Yes?" said another woman's voice. "Who is this?"

"Sorry," he said. "Wrong number."

"You kids get lost. You hear me? You just get lost."

"Sorry," he said again.

The guy behind us laughed. "You bitches lost?" he asked, smiling.

Francis put his finger on another broken word, "lco," and then he punched some more numbers into the keypad. The buzzer rang several times before a voice answered.

"What." A statement, not a question. A weary, thick voice. Then silence. That sort of silence that tells you somebody's listening.

"Hello?" Francis said into the intercom.

"I don't want none," said the man on the other end. "Whatever you're selling."

"No," said my brother. "I'm not selling anything. It's just me."

Stillness and silence. Even from the big guy behind us.

"It's me," said Francis. "It's us. Your sons."

Me and Francis, the guy in the lobby, we all waited for someone to speak. Someone to settle the matter.

"You've got the wrong place," said the man, and disconnected with a click.

———

We were driving back to Desirea's. The rain had stopped and the air was calm and strangely sweet. Francis reached down to the dashboard and the headlights snapped on.

"You're so quiet," he said.

"I'm just thinking."

I kept looking ahead. I felt his eyes on me.

"Why do you always have to be such a pussy?" he said.

FOUR

He arrives in our home like a ghost. Sits there, on the living room couch, being served tea by my mother as if this were the most ordinary thing in the world. He's as thin as before, wearing dark denims worn baggy and low without a belt, checkered underwear showing, a hood drawn over his head. He's got that onion-brown patch on his temple, that same forgotten continent. But he's changed. It isn't just the show of ten difficult years on his face. It's the loss and guilt that's palpable in him. Implicating.

"What's he doing here?" I whisper at Aisha.

We're in the kitchen, Aisha and I, fetching more crackers, more sugar and cream. Aisha seems, for the first time, a bit embarrassed. "I didn't actually think he'd come," she explains. "I sent a message through a friend. It wasn't even a real invitation, just a suggestion that we all meet up." She busies herself cutting thin slices of apple and cheese, putting them on crackers, adding a sprig of parsley. Hors d'oeuvres! She's serving a boy like Jelly *hors d'oeuvres*!

"He just showed up this morning when you were out," she continues explaining. "Your mother let him in. They've been talking."

I look back at Jelly and Mother on the couch. They don't seem to be talking at all. Jelly empties the container of cream into his cup after offering some to Mother. He pours sugar directly from the bowl. I catch him slipping a few of the crackers into his hoody pocket. Mother takes a delicate sip of her tea before appearing to ask Jelly a question, and he nods, still wearing headphones under his hood. I spot a foam mattress in the corner. A stuffed backpack sitting on top.

"This isn't a good idea, Aisha," I whisper. "I've warned you. I don't want Mother disturbed or confused. She's fragile."

"It's just temporary. He won't get in the way. Your mother was the one who suggested the mattress, and there's room. He said it'd be fine, he's crashed in far worse places. He doesn't have anywhere else to go."

"Where'd he come from? What does he do these days?"

"He does what we all do these days, Michael. He gets by."

I'm not satisfied by any of this. I watch as he removes his headphones and gently cups them over Mother's ears. He's still using a Walkman, old-school weirdo, and when he presses play she listens, her eyes widening, the sheer volume carrying as far away as the kitchen. Mother shakes the headphones off her head, smiling in a wrinkled-nose sort of way. He smiles back with teeth.

Jelly must sense my wariness towards him, because shortly after the tea, he leaves without a word. Through the window, I see him pass Mrs. Henry, who stops to stare before shaking her head and muttering something disapproving to the invisible congregation of souls forever accompanying her. If Jelly can hear the rebuke, he very wisely doesn't respond and continues walking down the avenue. He's taken his backpack, and for a moment I wonder if he's left for good. Should we have tried to talk? Ten years and not a single word between us. Should I at least have said goodbye? I feel more relief than guilt. But in a couple hours he returns with his backpack full, as well as two plastic bags of groceries in his hands. And there's another surprise.

He can cook.

He moves fluently through the inexpensive ingredients he's bought, bags of vegetables as well as dried peas, rice, little containers of seasonings he produces from his backpack. He chops like a chef, the sharp steel edge loud and quick upon the wood. Soon he's got the entire kitchen in chaos, no free space on the counters, all stove elements on. Mother has begun to pitch in too, and she sorts dried peas at the kitchen table, dropping them into a ceramic bowl with the sound of small pebbles. Even Aisha is participating, fetching pots and pans, washing vegetables in a big colander at the sink. I catch Jelly's eyes.

"Is that bodi?" I ask.

"Couldn't find it," he says. "Just string beans."

"We'll be ready to eat in a few minutes," says Aisha. "That right, Jelly?"

He nods and tilts a chopping board full of diced onions, garlic, and peppers towards a hot and oiled cast-iron pot. Instantly, there's a fierce scorching sound, the kitchen air quickly filling with a smell at once spiced and buttery and harsh. I've always had a weakness for fried hot peppers, Scotch bonnets in particular, and I feel my eyes tearing up. I do my best to swallow the tickling in my throat. I try holding my breath, but then blow out a loudly snotty bout of uncontrolled coughing. Aisha and Mother are laughing, but Jelly looks genuinely concerned.

"Maybe open the front door a bit?" he suggests.

"It's okay," I say, fighting for breath. "I have to leave now anyway."

I have another precious long shift at the Easy Buy, and I make sure to be on time. I perform a bunch of jobs, unloading skids, bagging groceries, cleaning up spills in aisles. Mr. Mississauga is with me again, and Manny tells us we need to unload the five skids at the back of the freezer section before we leave tonight. We bust our asses, and manage to finish, but then, just at the end of our shift, a stacked skid topples and a couple dozen cases of cola piss out their stickiness when they hit the floor. Mississauga sucks his teeth at me for the whole unpaid half-hour we're mopping up the mess. I'm in the staff dressing room, getting ready to head home, when Manny confronts me. But not about the cola.

"Heard you have a houseguest," he says.

"We're friends. She's just visiting."

"Not the girl, sly dog. Homeboy headphones, I mean."

"He's nobody," I say, hearing annoyance in my own voice. "A friend of my brother's. Your people in the Park got nothing better to do than spy on me?"

He begins a new lecture. There are *lowlifes*, he warns. There are people who attract all sorts of problems. I'm in no mood to listen, I'm sure my impatience shows on my face, and Manny's message gets more threatening. He warns that he can't employ someone who associates with criminals, degenerates. I nod, then walk out of the staff room, hurry through the empty aisles of the Easy, risking my job, I know, with this show of attitude. Manny follows, asking me if I ever look good and well at myself. When I step out into cold, he halts at the sliding doors.

"You ever actually *think* about your future?" he yells after me.

I spend a couple hours, maybe more, walking round and round the block, trying to think, trying to even name the emotions within me. I step into puddles of slush, heedless of the cold and wet. I cross the Lawrence Avenue bridge at least a half-dozen times, back and forth, getting splashed by cars. After an hour, my feet are stumps.

When I finally make my way to my block again, my head is foggy, but I notice, not far from our unit, the parked police car. When I open our front door, I see the whole living room and kitchen filled with strangers, mostly young people, standing about silently. I look about the room for Mother but I can't see her. It takes me only a moment more to notice the two figures in uniform standing inside. Suddenly too close, unreal, like a dream.

"Are you Michael?" asks one of the cops.

She's a woman with short blond hair, green eyes. She's young, maybe in her mid- to late twenties. Her name is

Bev, and I actually know her. She's a regular face in the Park. I've seen her talk down a drunk man when a confrontation could have easily escalated into violence. I've seen her chat casually with teenagers in the neighbourhood, really talk with them, not fish for information. She gets things, I know. She's a good cop, but none of this helps me right now. Every nerve in my body is alert. I can smell leather and a strong underarm deodorant from her partner, standing a few feet away. I can hear her creaks when she subtly adjusts her stance. Maybe the equipment on her belt, the black nightstick, the holstered gun.

"You're Michael, right?" she asks.

"Yes."

"Hi."

"Hi."

"We've had a noise complaint from your neighbour."

"Yes. Okay."

"We're just following up. Your friends have agreed to turn down the music."

"Okay."

"Are you all right, Michael?"

"Okay. Yes. I'm okay."

A noise complaint, nothing more. But I start when a metallic voice sounds over Bev's walkie-talkie, numbers being called out, an address. She says good night to me, and I watch both cops leave. I wait for the door to close behind them, I even peek through the curtains to see them walking to their car, before I turn to the crowd of strangers in my house.

They're younger than me, wearing the fashions, big and loose and colourful, of their time. Many are black and brown, but others are Asian, white, and who knows what else. They're beautiful, I can't help but see this even now. But right now they are intruders, *lowlifes*, entering without my permission, and attracting the attention of the authorities. They've been eating Jelly's food and leaving dirty plates scattered throughout the place, a fresh purple stain on the carpet right in front of the recliner. They've taken other liberties, resurrected Mother's old turntable, pulled out albums I haven't heard for ages. Aretha Franklin, Percy Sledge. *Nana Mouskouri*? Where the hell is my mother?

"Michael," says Aisha, appearing beside me, touching my arm. "Can I explain?"

I pull away because I've finally spotted her. She's wearing Jelly's Walkman, the headphones around her neck. She's sitting on the couch between Jelly and a big woman with hoop earrings. On the coffee table before them is a small green suitcase, the one Mother used decades ago to move to this country, the one she now uses to store pictures and memorabilia. Normally it's on a shelf high up in her closet. But it's been retrieved and opened wide for anyone to see. Pictures of Mother's life before this one. Pictures of me as a child. Pictures of

Francis. I push through the crowd towards Mother and grab her elbow to help her up from the couch, the photographs on her lap scattering to the floor.

"Michael," says Aisha, "what are you doing?"

I'm conscious, suddenly, of squeezing Mother's arm. She pulls hard away from my grip and smacks me across my face. For a moment, we stare at each other.

"We were . . . *listening* to music," she says. "We were . . . *talking*." Her voice cracks. She is shaking.

The attention of the whole room is upon me now. Anger on the face of the woman who'd been sitting beside Mother. Sadness on Jelly's. I turn to Aisha, still staring quietly at me.

"I warned you about strangers."

"These are my friends, Michael. They've heard the story and they want to know more. They want to show their respect."

"I don't want their respect. I want them out of this house."

As gently as I can, I take the ridiculous Walkman and headphones off Mother and throw them down on the couch. I take her hand and lead her through the crowd to her bedroom, closing the door behind us. Mother immediately goes to her bed, lies down with her eyes open. I try to touch her shoulder and she pulls away, the faint light from the street painting her face. I move closer to the door and stand listening to people in the living room asking questions in low voices, Aisha responding, and then the sounds of hasty tidying, furniture being moved around, hopefully back to its proper place. In time, I hear the sounds of people leaving.

When I'm sure everyone's gone, I gently close Mother's bedroom door behind me. The place is still a mess and the purple stain on the carpet looks permanent. Surprisingly, Jelly's Walkman is still on the couch, and I pick it up. I press play, listen to the whine of the machine, the slight sound of a voice, perhaps a man's, before putting on the headphones. I recognize the music from a barbershop a decade ago. Nina Simone, her opening to "Feeling Good." But changed, remixed, so that the band never arrives, the lonely voice forever looping back.

AFTER ANTON WAS KILLED, you could feel it more than ever. You caught in the eyes of strangers the suspicion or outright fear. You sensed the halo of menace above your head, glimpsed the turbulence swirling behind as you walked. On TV and in the papers, politicians promised to crack down on criminals, with echoed agreements from suited community spokesmen. But criminals weren't the only target. Every day, neighbourhood kids were stopped by the cops, the questions about their actions and whereabouts more probing. We were being watched by everyone, shopkeepers, neighbours, passersby. Maybe because he knew I was suffocating on my own, Francis, despite his disappointment with me after we tried to visit our father, made space for me to hang out with him at Desirea's.

The shop was Dru's, but it wasn't your typical business. Prospective clients were almost never welcomed. On my first afternoon, I watched a neighbourhood kid named Trance shyly enter the shop, produce nothing but pocket change and lint for a service that I observed was less of a haircut than a punishing rite of passage. Trance sat obediently in a barber's chair as Dru mercilessly went to work, pushing his head forward to buzz a neckline, yanking it to the side to reach that difficult spot behind the ears. Dru's thumb now digging into the poor boy's eye socket for steadiness. ("Of *course* you got nicked, fool! I *told* you not to move!") Most of the anger was show, and when it was over the kid was offered a beef patty and a Coke with the luxury of ice, and he was allowed to stay for the rest of the day.

When hanging out at Desirea's, I saw cash change hands, a modest income generated. But whether Dru willed it or not, the shop seemed to run on a different economy. In the thin light filtered and refracted through those untidy storefront windows, in the spell of Jelly's music, lives and names emerged. I watched a young man get a shave. He leaned way back in the chair, his eyes draped with a cloth, his cheeks and neck piled with lather. Jelly worked at his mixing board and turntables, and in that space of sound Dru used a straight razor, cutting a face out from underneath the white. And here, now, was Kev, who after his shave spent at least five minutes admiring the work in a mirror, then carefully adjusting his mesh-backed cap, the brim set perfectly flat and cocked to the right. Here too was big-boned Abdi, who every day requested "just a little touch-up." Here was Gene, a girl B-boy who sported the tightest fade. And here was the Professa, in his late twenties, his academic credentials uncertain, but always able to name the track Jelly was messing with.

"Otis Clay, 'A Lasting Love,'" he would announce, not even looking up from his copy of *The Source*.

Here was Raj, the Talker, and the only one among us lucky enough to live in a home his parents actually owned (or so he said). He wore a Kangol hat low over his eyes and a long chain of plated gold. He was a skinny guy, but he'd perfected a brawling posture that made him look bigger than he was, his arms propped out by the invisible bulk of his back and chest muscles. On my second day at Desirea's, he reluctantly confessed to having a rare medical condition. An elephantiasis of the penis, a burden that had nevertheless won him the tender sympathies of *several* ladies. Although, later that evening, when certain flesh-and-blood women came into the shop, Raj's tone suddenly changed. Carla, Yash, and Meeshi, official neighbourhood Beauties, their fingernails honed like weapons, their eyes squint-pools of steel. They sported designer jeans and bossy hairdos. In the suddenly quiet shop, they sat scowling, chewing gum, looking bored, waiting for something to happen. And during the hour the girls were there, Raj, the boy who'd once bragged magnificently about pussy, could barely get a sensible word out of his mouth.

"Um . . . like . . . you know . . . you girls want me to get you, like, a soda?"

Everyone laughed at Raj. Everyone laughed at each other. In Desirea's, you postured but you also played. You showed up every one of your dictated roles and fates. Our parents had come from Trinidad and Jamaica and Barbados, from Sri Lanka and Poland and Somalia and Vietnam. They worked shit jobs, struggled with rent, were chronically tired, and often pushed just as chronically tired notions about identity and respectability. But in Desirea's, different styles and kinships were possible. You found new language, you caught the gestures, you kept the meanings close as skin.

It was the Professa who first explained the music to me. That summer, rap went mainstream, sucking up all the attention of television and radio, of promoters and record labels, and suddenly all ears were on MCs. In the moneyed rush for the next big voice, the DJ was abandoned, his work onstage easily replaced by pre-recorded tracks and engineers working in studios. But as a result, something else became possible. The DJ, now fired from his day job as backup for the mike, was free to return to the origins, to *the materials*. Old heroes like DJ Kool Herc were remembered, and a new generation of innovators was left to experiment on their own.

Almost every day, Francis and Jelly brought in a new crate of records scavenged from garages and second-hand shops. They would carefully assess their finds, nudging shoulders, touching hands, laughing quietly to each other over some cheesy album covers water-blistered or faded with time. They would pull out the vinyl, use a soft cloth to gently wipe the surface, check for scratches in good light, and then cue the record up. They'd make all the boys in the shop listen, at first just listen, without messing with things. We heard, as if with new ears, the music of our parents, the lost arts of funk especially, but also ska and soul, blues and jazz. We heard an album by Toots and the Maytals, "borrowed" from a parent whose musical tastes you would never think to trust. We heard Coltrane as if for the first time. (What the *fuck*, whispered little Trance. *Language*, bitch! scolded Dru.) We listened patiently to Satchmo and Aretha Franklin, Marley and Harry Belafonte, stuff too sweetly familiar from TV commercials and movie soundtracks. But Francis and Jelly stole it all back for us, the dead and the living, made it ours to listen to, before Jelly went to work.

He spent hours every day at his set-up of Technics 1200s, the turntables easily the most expensive things in the shop, and probably in our lives. With a headphone on one ear, his fingers moving from mixing board to the twinned vinyl, he'd discover and isolate the break beat, that precious particle of meaning, that three-second glimpse of the bigger story of a song, extending now forever. Jelly was a master at this, and he could also scratch as good as anyone we'd heard. But he was weird even among the new class of DJs, for his genius was all about continuous flow, about ceaselessly mixing in one sound, one style, one *era* with another. He worked magic with the cross-fader and the different equalizers, allowing us to recognize connections we'd never otherwise imagine. Between ska and blues. Between Port of Spain and Philadelphia. Between the 1950s and the late 1980s. Sometimes it failed, and the noise had no resonance. Even I could understand that. Other times it worked, the old and elsewhere summoned back and enthroned in an amplified rhythm that sent everyone in the shop suddenly pouting and nodding and calling back.

"That's brilliant, Jelly," said Raj. "You're a . . . what do they call it now? A *metaphysician*. A goddamned *metaphysician*!"

"I predict multitudinous felicitations at the Ex," said the Professa.

I learned it then, their big plan. A major hip-hop concert at the CNE was just days away. Big names and acts were coming from the cities that mattered, New York and L.A. At the promotional events leading up to the concert, there'd be talent scouts and official auditions, and record deals might be on offer. The world-famous artist the Conductor would be there. And this would be the chance for Jelly to take stage and shine, to represent.

"So true," said Raj. "You're going to kill it at the Ex."

"It's true," Francis said to Jelly, touching hands and pulling him close. "We're gonna do it."

Francis had always before played cool and sensible. He protected himself, the way you had to. But now I glimpsed in him not only a strange and dangerous hope but also something else. There is a thing that sometimes happens between certain neighbourhood boys. It shows itself, this thing, in touched hands, in certain glances and embraces, its truth deep, undeniable, but rarely spoken or explained. Sometimes never even truly spotted. Although now, in the midst of my own thing, I could see.

"You're going to do this," Francis said, his hand on Jelly's neck.

Her father was working late shifts that August, and so, for the first time, Aisha invited me to her home. Even though the sun had set, their unit was still hot, with only one source of light from the stove risked. So much in their home reminded me of mine. The neatness, the patterned chesterfield, the glass bowl of lentils set out in the kitchen to soak for the next day's meal, the used tea bag kept on a square of foil for a second use. There were photos of Aisha receiving one award or the other. There was a shelf of books, and also a record player with albums.

"Look," she said, sitting with me on the chesterfield. "We've really got to talk about your hair. What are you doing exactly? No, what are you *trying* to do?"

"It's, you know, a hi-top fade."

"You look like Gumby. A flop-head Gumby."

"Francis used to pull it off."

"Well you're not Francis, now, are you?"

She went on laughing for a bit. She told me that when she used to sit in her enrichment classes, the girls would spend a third of their time on the composition and calculus, and two-thirds of their time talking about Francis. "The stuff that came out of their mouths," she said. "I'm talking *predatory*, Michael. I don't care what reputation for toughness your brother has, he wouldn't stand a chance with those girls. They'd eat him alive. They'd kill, even now, for an introduction."

"Would you like an introduction too?" I asked quietly.

She stopped laughing, and her smile seemed to change.

"What?" I asked.

"Well?" she answered.

She took me to her bedroom, which was also neat, which also contained books, and she shut the door behind us. Without warning, she lifted off my shirt and then did the same with her own. She pushed down her shorts and did the same to me, and we stood there for a moment. She was beautiful, but when she came closer I flinched. She drew my hand towards her body, and I found the scar near the bottom her stomach that might have been an appendix operation, the first part of her I touched.

Somewhere, in the back of my mind, I understood that I was supposed to be good at this, was supposed to know, instinctively, what to do. But I didn't. We lay together on the bed for a long time, learning how to touch and kiss each other. She gently pushed my head lower down her body, and afterwards she found protection, which I fumblingly put on inside out. She nodded at me and kept her eyes open when I entered her, and she turned her face away, and when she turned back her eyes were closed and her mouth reached up for mine.

Later, she guided my hand to where it needed to be, and in the end helped herself, and afterwards we lay on the bed without speaking. It was not her first time, and when I kissed her fingers gently, over and over again, she had her own smell upon them.

IT IS NOW TWO HOURS AFTER the last of the partygoers left, and while Mother sleeps in her room I've been cleaning the kitchen and living room. I've opened the windows to let the smoke out, put furniture back where it belongs. It's all still a mess. Crumbs scattered all about, but I'll wait until morning to vacuum. Bottles of wine and beer have been abandoned, and I've helped myself to them. Mother's suitcase is still yawning open on the coffee table, and only now, with drink in me, do I permit myself a look.

Old things. Things to remember, and maybe, just as much, things to forget. Postcards and concert tickets. Mementoes and relics. A small maroon box filled with glass jewellery, pretty but worthless. There are many photographs, of course, some loose and some bound together with paper clips and elastics, pictures of Mother and me and Francis, but I try to ignore them. I instead take out the school notebook that Mother has for some reason saved from her childhood. It has the meaningless title of *Standard A* on the cover, and inside are words written so beautifully and carefully, as if, for the girl who wrote them, absolutely everything were at stake.

Daffodil.

Rochester.

Empire.

Preposterous.

Beside each word is a quick check mark, and then a brief note at the end of the page. "Very good," it says.

I'm still sitting on the couch when Aisha returns alone around one, using her own key. I signal that Mother is sleeping in her room, and she comes in slowly. I ask her where Jelly is, and she says he's getting something for the carpet stain. He'll be back in a moment, just to pick up his stuff if he has to go. I don't respond. I'm not going to be moved right now by pity. She joins me on the far end of the couch, but she reaches closer for the photographs I've laid out, relatives from the village where her own father was born. She finds a picture of Mother as a teenager in a dress maybe blue or green, her eyes looking strangely into the distance, her thin arm held up against the power of the sun.

"She was beautiful, Michael," she says. "She still is. Do you know about the white building in the background? Did you go when you visited? It's the church of the Spiritual Baptists. Shouter Baptists, they used to be called. I learned about them when I was there. For a long time, their services were outlawed in Trinidad. They couldn't worship the way they chose to. They couldn't praise and weep loudly."

Her brow is furrowed and she's making a sound in her throat like difficult swallowing. She's crying, I know, but when I touch her shoulder she shakes her head angrily. She clears her throat and swallows. When she speaks again, her voice is hoarse.

"My father lived only a short walk away from that church, but he told me nothing about it. He told me so little about his past. He didn't mention how his parents couldn't always feed their children. He never mentioned his dead brother and dead sister, both taken in childhood, or that his aunt had "entertained" American soldiers to survive. He never explained why he worked his whole life here as a security guard. Even his cancer was something I had to learn, too late, from a nurse."

I can see him now. It was the winter before that last summer, and I was returning home when I saw Francis standing with Samuel on the sidewalk near the Waldorf. When I got near, my brother gave me a tight nod, but Samuel smiled, took off his hat, and smoothed his sparse and greying hair. "Good evening," he said. And then, incredibly, he started to sing. He sang, badly and in a lowered voice, and it was a song in French, I could remember that much, but I couldn't name it, and anyway my attention was all on Francis. It'd been a difficult week, and my brother had been quarrelling with Mother again. He could be set off, I knew, by anything offered from an adult, anything perceived as educated posturing or veiled mockery. But as Samuel sang, all my brother did was stare out at the street, awkward, even a bit shy. The singing lasted only for a few seconds. It was an in-joke of sorts, I assumed, but Samuel seemed to recognize that Francis wasn't enjoying the experience. He glanced at me, and with a quick nod, politely took his leave.

I want to tell Aisha about this moment. I want the sort of conversation I've hoped to have with her since she's come back. But now I hear footsteps on the porch and see the front door opening. It's Jelly. He's carrying a spray bottle of stain remover. He closes the door behind him but remains standing on the doormat, as if unwilling to step in farther. Aisha smiles, beckons him in, and he removes his shoes, goes to the kitchen to wet a cloth and then over to the stain to gingerly test for dampness. He reads the instructions on the spray bottle, squinting at the fine print.

Aisha huffs a laugh through her nose. She gets up from the couch and goes into my bedroom. Jelly has begun spraying and scrubbing at the stain when she returns with a light green flyer. It features the image of a microphone set up on a stage. And over this is a list of performers. Jah-Righteous, Sister Sojourner, Dutty Bookman. Second from the bottom: DJ Djeli.

"*Djeli*," Aisha says. "As in a griot. A storyteller with memory. A few days after my father's death, I was downtown, just walking, mourning, pretty out of it still. I heard someone call from behind me, 'Yo, sister,' and when I turned, a boy nervously offered this flyer. He apologized for shouting out. He suggested that I help spread the word, 'You know, like, maybe if you have a son or daughter or something.' Blind little fuck."

"It was Scott," says Jelly. "Such a good kid. He meant no offence."

"Well, I guess I wasn't looking my best," says Aisha. "Anyway, I took the flyer, but wondered why I did. And why the next night I showed up at that tiny basement club in the city. There were maybe three dozen of the expected sorts, students, artists, activists, nobodies. There was music, some good, some not so very good. There was poetry, some good, some not so good. But I enjoyed myself. I felt connected somehow."

I look at the name once more. *Djeli*. Did the boys at Desirea's always mean it this way? Did they know? I look at Jelly, still scrubbing, seemingly only spreading the purple wider on the carpet. He sighs.

"I don't have to stay," he says.

"Look," I say. "I'm sorry I got angry. I get what you were all trying to do. You both can stay another night if you need, okay? I'm just trying to warn you that we have to go slow with Mother. It's not easy for her. She's broken. Really broken."

Aisha nods. She shuffles through the photographs still in her hand and finds one of Francis from the late '70s. It shows my brother in an Afro and a wide-collared shirt, grass green and orange. She shows the picture to Jelly. The look I caught earlier in the night returns. A sadness implicating.

THE NIGHT AFTER AISHA AND I first touched, the boys at Desirea's decided Jelly needed a dress rehearsal, a practice throw-down, with a real audience. Aisha and I walked together through the trashed-up glare of the avenue, the night heat raw upon our skins. As soon as we reached the back of the strip mall, we could see and hear it, light and music radiating through the overlapping flyers and leaflets posted all over the windows. I pulled open the door to find a press of people inside. Dru let Aisha in, but then put out his arm to block me.

"ID, please," he said.

"Screw off," I said.

"You watch your fucking language, young man."

Desirea's had transformed, amazingly, into something like a club, with borrowed speakers and amplifiers and mikes. Thin cloths were draped over lamps, creating coloured shadows over everything. Jelly was doing his thing with mixers and turntables on a makeshift raised stage, and the crowd was rocking bold and free and close to one another. Some boy I didn't recognize was saying something into a jacked-in mike, and a big girl, hair done up Golden Beauty, snatched the mike away. "Give it here," the boy said, but she ignored him, and other girls cheered. Golden Beauty spoke into Jelly's ear, and he nodded and found her a break beat. You could see her lips moving for a while as she rehearsed a few lines in her head, and then she started rhyming in a sharp, high voice, hands carving out words in the air.

"Youth of Eglinton,

"Youth of Kingston,

"Youth of Compton,

"Youth of Brooklyn,

"Youth of Scarborough . . ."

I saw Francis next to Jelly as his man switched up the music, knitting together two completely different tracks, old and new, Caribbean and American and now African soul, and then a cheer rising from the crowd.

Francis calling out "Volume!" and others joining the call. And now Aisha too, sweeping her hair from her face, and saying, "Volume!" Every voice in the place together.

Volume!

FIVE

Around six o'clock in the morning, just as that party at Desirea's was winding down, the cops showed up. Visits to Desirea's had happened before, according to the boys. And there was at least a routine to these intrusions. But this time, in the wake of the shootings and resulting crackdown, the cops were cold-eyed with purpose. They appeared in force at the front door, six of them at once in bulky vests, and when they asked to be let in we understood that it wasn't really a request. They entered our space and the shop suddenly became small, the air changed. The music was cut, the faces of the crowd once glowing now expressionless.

"What's this about?" asked Dru.

"A neighbour smelled pot," explained a cop. "We're searching for drugs."

"Might I suggest an office on Bay Street?"

"Stand by the wall, funnyman. Empty your pockets. The rest of you too."

Everyone started moving slowly to the wall, but one cop didn't like the way Jelly was dawdling at his turntable, taking two of his precious records off the turntables and putting them into their sleeves. The cop moved over to him, tapped him hard. "Hey, *genius*," he said.

Francis jerked around. "Don't touch him!" he shouted.

A dangerous moment of quiet in Desirea's. Everyone, even the police, silent and staring. I felt a single cold itch of sweat creep down the back of my shirt. The cop who had touched Jelly looked younger than the rest.

"Excuse me?" he asked, a smile on his face.

Francis didn't answer, and his stare grew hard and unblinking, moisture rimming his eyes. I stared helplessly at the hand of the younger cop and its distance to the holstered gun on his belt. An impossibly long period of time until the cop asked again, "Excuse me?" and then an older cop said something to him under his breath.

"Okay, *Francis*," the younger cop returned. "You and

your friend move over there to the wall. Empty your pockets like the rest."

My brother and Jelly obeyed. And the search proceeded quickly. There was little to find. A roach clip was discovered in the Professa's pocket, which Dru quickly explained was, in fact, a hair clip, and proceeded to demonstrate this on a boy with dreads, who promptly slapped it out of his hands and gave him a look. The older cop rolled his eyes but didn't call anyone out. When the search was finished, he thanked us for allowing his crew to enter.

"Oh no," Dru said. "Thank *you*, good officers."

For a few seconds after the cops left, no one in the shop moved or spoke. I stared at Francis, still wet-eyed and shaking, with fear or anger or both. And only when Jelly approached him and touched his arm did he swallow thickly and nod.

Francis could be pushed. Everyone knew it. It was a sense you had, growing up in the Park, a sense famously confirmed one evening when Francis was sixteen. It was the week before Christmas, and Mother had just come home from work. She had put on lipstick and the pleated skirt she sometimes wore on "occasions." She was humming a bit of parang, the Spanish-sounding music we knew was played at this time of year in Trinidad, and she seemed happy, or at least determined to be. She quickly reheated and served what remained of yesterday's lentil stew, and when Francis said, "You're hardly leaving any for yourself," she claimed she wasn't hungry. She then warned us it was probably going to be a quiet Christmas this year, one with a nice meal but perhaps no gifts. It was just "the economy," she explained. She would find new work and hopefully get overtime hours after the holidays.

Sitting at the table, Francis got quiet, and that was all, just quietness.

Mother at first just continued humming. Then she put down her fork, shut her eyes in anger. "Grow up," she whispered. "Be a man."

Francis stayed quiet for a bit longer, and then he rose and began putting on his coat. I rushed to put on my own jacket and followed him out the door.

A sleety rain was blowing hard against our faces, the sky the bitter colour of road salt. Francis and I walked twenty minutes to the nearest 7-Eleven, but after we bought a hot dog each and ate them inside, the security guard said we'd have to go or else he'd call the cops. We ended up walking to a bus shelter a block away, and we sat shivering inside on the bench without saying anything. We stared at the dripping doorway, our hands in our pockets, our necks and cheeks hunched into our coats, our hands pulled into our sleeves for warmth. My shoes were soaked, and I kept curling and uncurling my toes to keep them from freezing.

A woman stepped into the shelter. She was nicely dressed, despite the weather, and she was carrying shopping bags that had coloured ropes for handles. She obviously hadn't seen Francis and me through the grime-streaked glass of the shelter, and now that she found herself in close quarters with us, she looked a bit uncomfortable. Francis was taking up two spaces on the bench, and he moved so she could sit, but she looked deliberately away. He tried to catch her eye, and even at one point gestured to the available seat, but this only seemed to scare her more. She left, walking down the street, maybe to the next shelter, her heels clicking on the sidewalk.

"It's not Mother's fault," I said. "She's doing her best."

"I know it's not her fault, shithead! What kind of guy do you think I am?"

A group of youths approached the shelter. They were hard to recognize at first, but they were bigger than us. They were dressed in heavy oversized shirts and loose jeans that hung out from the bottoms of their unbuttoned coats. One stood up on the pedals of a bike that was way too short for him, the handlebars done up with ragged black tape. They were lit hard from behind by the caged security light on the back of an apartment building so that as they approached they seemed to have no faces, just darkness outlined by glare.

"We should go," I said to Francis.

"Nobody owns a bus shelter," said Francis.

It wasn't the right time to fight over the question, but I stayed, hoping that the group would just pass us by. Instead they crowded at the doorway, blocking us from leaving. Up close, they weren't so menacing. They were people we knew, neighbourhood boys who had learned to carry themselves tough. One of them flicked a lighter, and a huge orange flame lit the other smiling faces while the shadows danced and quivered on the glass of the shelter. The smallest, a youth who called himself Scatter, wore shades that gave him reflective bug eyes. A wicked smile when he saw me.

"What's up, bitch?" he said.

There was laughter then. Mean and throaty laughter. One kid showed a big white wad of gum in his mouth. Another one was missing a bunch of his front teeth, though he must have been fourteen at least. Then the laughter faded and there was an awkward pause when I guess I was supposed to answer.

"Hey, bitch," said Scatter. "Hey, faggot. I just addressed you and shit."

"Sup," I told him, carefully.

"Sup, he tells me," Scatter said, laughing. "*Sup*."

Francis had warned me to stand up for myself. You just need to do it once, he had said. And in that bus shelter, he was watching me, waiting for me to act. I could feel the taffy in my stomach pulling, churning. Under my breath, I told Scatter to fuck off. A couple of the bigger youths chuckled, and there was a quick show of surprise on Scatter's face, an embarrassed glance to his friends, before he recovered. He put on his own smile, as if he had been waiting for this. And then he drew from his coat a knife.

It was a hunting knife of some sort, the kind you see advertised on late-night TV, its blade shining blue in the light. Scatter held it at me, the tip of the blade low, out of sight of most people on the street, almost now touching my groin.

"Like that?" he asked.

I was ready to mumble something, not an apology, but something to try to defuse the situation, but then Francis, without taking his eyes off Scatter, slowly brought his hand up to the knife and clasped his fingers around the naked blade.

He reached and closed his hand around the weapon.

For seconds there was struggle as the two boys stared at each other. In the end, Francis was left holding the knife in his bloodied hand. And if Scatter's face momentarily showed shock, maybe even concern, this quickly vanished. He huffed a laugh through his nose, and backing casually away, he gave voice to all of the other quiet witnesses, even me.

"Fucking *crazy*," he said.

Both Scatter and Francis earned reputations after that. The one holding the handle of the knife had ultimately proved himself unable to let the cutting continue. Even with his clear advantage of grip, Scatter had let go of the knife, and this display of weakness cost him, regardless of his efforts, through increasing postures and acts of aggression, to correct it.

But the one holding the blade earned something very different. And in the many retellings of the story, Francis's hand was not just cut but gashed to the bone, red ropes of blood falling to the ground. Francis proved that with one gesture, you could forever confirm a reputation. Not only that he could stand his ground but that he could, when pushed, go mad.

On the evening of Jelly's audition, Francis touched up his fade in the mirror for a good hour, and even in the heat, he insisted on wearing a thin black jacket with a fur collar. He rolled his eyes at the two-toned do-rag on my head, but he didn't say anything.

The plan was to meet most of the boys from Desirea's at the concert site itself. Francis would be driving. After we collected the car from the barbershop, we made a stop at the Waldorf, to pick up Aisha. She wore her ordinary clothes, but also a cap, the only concession she would make to anything like a B-girl style. She squeezed into the back with me. We drove to a "good" part of the suburb, one with detached homes, to pick up Raj from his parents' place. He was dressed in a bright yellow track suit, a two-legged banana, but when he saw my own attempt at an outfit, he glared.

"No way," he said to my brother. "*Him*? You brought him with you?"

"Just relax," my brother said. "He'll be cool."

"What the hell is that thing he's wearing?"

"What are you talking about?" I said.

"That thing on your head. You look like bloody Aunt Jemima!"

We picked up Jelly last from his building, a low-rise named the Rosedale. The building slanted as if it were leaning into the soft and grassless ground. The front yards were muddy lengths of earth, and there were rusted cars on cinder blocks, a mush of old pizza boxes, clotheslines with dirty-looking clothes on them. Jelly was waiting outside with a little kid who might have been his brother. They bumped fists and hugged, and the kid watched, waving again, as Jelly lugged a crate of records to the car. When we pulled away, the kid yelled "Good luck!" but Jelly didn't look back. He was wearing his same thin grey hoody. He kept looking nervously at his fingers, but when he caught me looking he hid them under his arms.

"Okay," he said, suddenly. "Let's do this."

When we reached the Ex, we parked and met up with the rest of the crew and walked as cool as possible to the stadium. There were some posters up of the performers flanked by women in tight shorts and bras and sporting glittering chains and bracelets. There was already a long lineup for the auditions, which led to a tent off to the side. We took our spot at the end of the line, which crawled slowly towards a group of bouncers checking ID and taking names. Pulsing music in the air.

The wait felt like forever, and already this was an irritation. Every once in a while we'd hear some music start up from inside the audition tent, some kid throwing down for a while, and then the music would suddenly cut, maybe because the time was up or the patience of the listeners was spent. I was stuck right behind some middle-class white kids wearing the sort of gear hardly anybody could afford. Nikes, Air Jordans, Louis Vuitton. They joked around, making gang signs with their fingers. They complained about some of the acts. "Watered-down sell-out crap," said one. "Now *Frontman*, he's the real shit. Nigga actually did time in jail for *assault* and shit."

I was standing with Aisha, and I twice caught her looking at Francis, who was fidgeting, craning his neck to attempt to see into the tent, or else checking again and again the crate of records Jelly had brought. The shadows of game booths and rides at the Ex were lengthening, and the sky behind the monster rides turned burnt orange.

Finally, we were within sight of the bouncers. They were all beefy and tall, and they wore T-shirts that read "Regal Sport," one of the event's main sponsors.

"The stage looks clear now," Francis told them.

"Relax, guy," answered one of the bouncers. "You'll get your turn."

"Okay," said another. "You superstars are in next."

A stage was already set up with turntables, a mixing board, and speakers. In front of the stage was a table with five chairs, but only two guys were sitting there. One, probably a promoter, was dressed in a white shirt, but the other was the Conductor, dressed in chains and a black blazer, loud white Jordans on his feet. As we entered, White Shirt kept talking to him as if we didn't exist, but the Conductor nodded at us and gestured to the stage. Jelly lugged his crate of records to the turntables, and Francis helped him set up, adjusting the headphones, testing the sound, angling a number of records out of the crate so they could be seized when needed. They had Technics 1200s in the battle position, and a mixing board with more dials, switches, and stuff than even Jelly had probably ever seen before. There was a moment when they were ready, and they both looked at the judges and the rest of us watching, and then at each other. They didn't touch hands. Francis just nodded and stepped back.

It began, surprisingly, with voice. Once before, in Desirea's, Jelly had played from a cassette tape something that had stumped even the Professa. It was in a language I didn't recognize, and when it was over Francis said it was *balwo*, a style of singing from

Somalia, and usually about love. And now Jelly played it again, letting the words ring in the empty air for almost ten seconds before he went to work. A drum and bass line was added, and then, seamlessly, relentlessly, other music was layered in. Soul, rocksteady, even calypso and Congolese rhumba. Francis was passing and grabbing records when needed. I heard artists that the Professa had already named for me: Gladys Knight, Smokey Robinson, Etta James. I heard tabla and the silly of disco. I heard a guitar lick from Hendrix. A blues rift sped up into a digital future. He overlaid voices on top of one another, messed with time, and made a man sound like a woman and a woman like a man, the truer feeling and meaning of a song suddenly emerging through the work of his hands.

"*Shit*," whispered Raj, standing beside me.

We were stilled. It was more than we had imagined, bigger and wilder. *Weirder*, even for Jelly. Nothing seemed beyond his reach. Country western, punk. The Conductor was all attention. Styles and voices bled together, music tunnelled into noise into music into noise. White Shirt waved for it all to stop, but Jelly was too zoned in to stop. He woke only when Francis touched his shoulder, and then he dialed everything down, lifted the needles.

The boys rushed to Jelly to congratulate him, while Francis stood aside, breathing heavily, a smile on his face. The Conductor was standing and clapping, and when he could be heard he thanked Jelly and the crew for the sample, said it was great, that Jelly had real talent. He told us to keep the peace and to stay in school, and then he and White Shirt went back to talking. We all stood there waiting for something more, but I wasn't sure what. Finally, Francis spoke up.

"Do you want hear some more from him?" he asked.

"Thank you," said White Shirt, without even looking at him.

"He could do another set, really quick."

"Thank you. There's another group waiting."

Francis continued standing there. The boys from Desirea's were now gesturing at him to come along. White Shirt turned to a switchboard technician and gave a "what the fuck?" look.

Francis cleared his throat. "So you're going to contact us if we win?" he asked.

"Yeah, kid. Sure. We'll definitely contact you."

We'd already planned to celebrate that night at Desirea's, and Dru said he'd better get back to help set up. Gradually, the boys started to leave, each giving props to Jelly before heading off.

"Monumental," said the Professa.

Aisha gave me a hug and said she probably couldn't meet up at Desirea's. "It was great," she said to both Jelly and Francis. "That's the truth. It doesn't really matter what a promoter thinks. You've already won." But I thought her voice sounded a bit too gentle, and Francis just swallowed and nodded. We were left, Francis, Jelly, and me, and it all seemed to suddenly catch up with my brother: the sleepless nights after the shootings and before the audition, the sheer expectation reduced to a single performance quickly cut off. Francis agonized that the set-up had been all wrong, the turntables were positioned too high and didn't seem calibrated, the needle wasn't on point, they never gave us enough time.

"Will they even know how to find us?" he said. "Do they have our contact info? Did anybody see them even write it down?"

Jelly shrugged. The lineup had disappeared now, and the bouncers were still outside the audition tent, joking around. Aside from them, no one else was around, except for some cleaning staff, picking up all the trash left outside. Francis looked back at the tent and the bouncers and then started walking in their direction. Jelly and I followed.

There were four of them outside now, one black and three white, and at first they ignored us. But then one tapped the other and they all turned to look.

"I need to talk to the promoter," Francis said.

"Sorry, guy. Show's over."

"We just need to talk with him."

"You heard me, guy. You ain't getting in."

They were crowding in front of him, and they were huge, professionally huge, full of weight-gaining powders. "Regal Sport" blaring on their chests. Francis stepped closer, staring, and suddenly everything felt very tense.

"Listen to me," explained Francis. "We were just in there."

"Oh, you was just in there," said the black bouncer.

"We were auditioning. We were performing."

"Oh I see, you guys were *performing*," the bouncer said. "You was doing your thing? You and your *homies*? Your niggaz?" He crippled up his hands into some fake gesture. The white bouncers laughed.

Jelly touched Francis's shoulder, but Francis shrugged his hand away. Jelly touched him again, this time gently on his arm, whispering something, but my brother didn't respond. The bouncers continued to laugh. I could see Francis's eyes start to tear up. He swallowed.

"We're going in," he said.

"I don't think so," said the black bouncer.

"Francis . . ." I said.

"Yeah, *Francis*, how about you listen to the little bitch there—"

The punch hit the bouncer hard on the nose, a sick crunch, and he stumbled back. The fight started immediately. In situations like this, when it's desperate and you've probably got no chance at all, you've got to go all in. Jelly probably knew this best, because we both did our best, swinging wildly at the bouncers. Jelly at least seemed to connect, but my knuckles barely glanced against anything before I was hit heavily, my jaw smashed bad to a numbness not a pain. I was struck twice in the ribs with something that felt like a bat before being put in some sort of hold. My shoulder was tearing, and I could do nothing but watch two bouncers beat on my brother. They'd kicked his legs out from under him, and he was on the ground trying to protect his head from fists and boots.

"Fucker broke my nose . . ." said one bouncer.

"Hold him down," said another.

"Fuck him up. Do his face."

Jelly had been put in an arm hold too, and he was screaming as the bouncers kept kicking Francis in the stomach, face, standing on his fingers. I heard other sounds coming from my brother, grunts and swearing, a sound like a stick hitting a sack of wet sand. I heard strained sounds made by his mouth and lungs, but no words. I heard myself saying *stop*. My mouth now filled thick with salt.

It did stop. A man was shouting something. It took some time before the words became clear, and for me to realize that it was a man calling from the tent. Francis was quiet, curled away from me.

I saw the bouncers walk back to the tent. Francis got to his feet, but he looked dazed, haunted, as if he didn't know exactly where he was or what had happened. Jelly tried to steady him, but my brother again shrugged him off. I got up last, wincing at the pain in my ribs. Francis was spitting blood and softly chanting nonsense, and Jelly spoke to him through what sounded like mashed lips. Francis bent, holding his sides, to pick his cap up from the ground. He brushed it carefully and put it on. We began limping away.

"You there!"

It was White Shirt. He was standing at the entrance to the tent. He was gesturing at us with his phone.

"You come back here and I'll call the police," he said. "Do you understand? I'll have you thugs arrested."

My ribs ached when I breathed, and when I ran my tongue over my lip it tasted like liver and didn't feel like part of me. My mouth filled with liquid salt. But it was Francis who looked ruined. His left eye was swollen shut and leaked a thin fluid. His nose was a mess, and his lips were torn. The blood kept coming from his nose, and he kept wiping it away with the bottom of his shirt.

Jelly helped him get into the car. He even ridiculously put on his seat belt. Jelly wanted to take him to a hospital, but Francis kicked up a fuss. "No way," he said. "They'll bust us for fighting. No *way*." We stopped at a gas station to use the brushed-steel mirror in the washroom to clean up. But we were interrupted by an attendant who, standing at a safe distance, said he'd call the cops if we didn't push off.

Jelly pulled out into the street again. "I'll clean him up at Desirea's. With the rest of the boys."

"No," I said. "Please, just drop us both at home."

"He needs our help. He needs his people."

"I'll go home first," said Francis. "My hat?" he asked, but it was already on his head.

Mother stood up from her seat on the couch. She was dressed for bed but sharpened immediately, staring at her eldest son with widened eyes in the blue and flickering light of the television.

"Francis!" she said.

He stumbled towards her. She closed her eyes while she held him, and then gently pushed him away to look at his face, her nose flaring. We'd done our best, but he still looked a mess. Mother used the sleeve of her own bathrobe to gently wipe at the sweat and crusted blood on his face. My brother wore a look of pure sorrow.

"Francis, what happened to you?"

She pulled him close, said she was going to get him help. Whatever it was, whatever he'd done, she was going to get the right help, she promised. He started to make low moaning sounds, deep within his stomach. He began whispering apologies to her for everything, for his face, for his blood upon her clean nightdress, for the hard work she'd always had to do.

"Hush, my son. Stop speaking. Please stop crying."

"I'm sorry, Mother."

"Hush now. Sit here on the couch, Francis. Please just stay still. I'm not leaving you, I promise. I'm getting things for you. Gauze, ointment."

"I'm so very sorry about everything," he said.

She hurried to the bathroom, and I heard her open the cabinet behind the mirror, rummage through the shelves, the metallic sounds of things falling into the sink. I went into the bathroom to help. I put away the toiletries that she knocked down. I held her shaking hands and told her that it'd be all right, and she closed her eyes and spent a moment steadying herself. But when we both returned to the living room, Francis was gone.

"PLEASE," AISHA WHISPERS TO ME. "You have to get up."

I'm in the living room, on the couch, and in the same clothes I've worn since returning from work to break up the party. It feels like early morning but it's very dark, the room cold, a sleet blowing noisily against the windows.

Aisha crouches beside me. "There's been an accident."

"What? Where . . . Who?"

"Your mother. She was wandering across the avenue. Jelly with her."

She's saying something more to me, but I don't hear. I'm up so quickly that I'm dizzy, stamping on my shoes. In the rightmost lane of the avenue, I see cars parked with their headlights shining upon a small group of neighbours, a man standing before them to wave away traffic. I run closer and see Mother on the ground. She is wearing a nightdress that is wet from the road, and I pull the material lower over her legs. She is breathing. Her right leg looks swollen and badly bruised, and her eyes are pressed tight, signalling that she is conscious. Jelly is by her head, whispering to her.

"I witnessed it," says Mrs. Henry to me. "I saw his car strike her."

"She just stepped out onto the road," says a man. "I couldn't stop in time."

He's not from here. He's well dressed, his car is big and expensive. "She stepped into the road out of nowhere," he repeats. A neighbour says they've called an ambulance, and now I hear the siren. I look down at Mother and see Jelly dabbing at her mouth with a tissue.

"Don't touch her!" I shout.

"She's thirsty," Jelly says.

"I said don't fucking touch her."

Jelly stands, watching me, and Mrs. Henry shoulders her way past me. She bends with difficulty down to Mother and touches her face. "Ruth?" she asks calmly. "You will be all right." She starts to sing softly with closed

136

eyes. "Come home, Zion wanderer. Come home, Zion wanderer." Mother nods, eyes closed too.

The ambulance arrives and the paramedics put Mother onto a stretcher, put a mask on her face. They ask me if I'll ride in the back with her, but I can't seem to answer them.

"Jelly and I will meet you at the hospital," Aisha breaks in.

"Stay away from us!" I shout.

"Michael," she begins.

"I mean it."

The paramedic asks again if I'm riding in the back, and I get in and the doors shut and protect me from their faces.

Mother is taken quickly away from me, and a nurse is asking me questions about her. Do you have her health card number? Has she been ill? Is she on any medications? Does she have a history of mental illness, confusion, dementia? I think I've been shaking my head, but I don't know. The buzzing tubes above me cast chemical white light and throw no shadows, and I look up to them and listen for a short while. The nurse speaks slower now. There may be shock, there may be broken bones, but for now my mother looks stable. They may want to keep her here for observation. I'll be able to see her soon, but it may be a long night. I should make myself comfortable.

The waiting area features a vinyl couch and a rubber plant and a box of Kleenex on a side table. There's a television mounted on the wall, and I watch commercials for cars and vegetable slicers and vitamin formulas. A man with a trimmed beard who's willing to sell you calcium and zinc, shark cartilage and rosehips, secret cures for those you love.

Some time had passed. How much time, I don't know. I'm looking at the closing credits of an action film when a big man in a uniform appears beside me. It takes me embarrassingly long to realize he's a nurse. He's smiling kindly. "Are you Mrs. Joseph's son?" I nod, and he tells me that her right leg has been set, complex, but not terrible. Her hip appears fine, thank goodness, but she is not responding to any of their questions, and they're not sure if she's in any pain still. He wants to know if I can help them in some way, and I nod, but can't find my voice or the right words. I touch the wet on my face, and the man nods and puts his hand warm upon my arm. He asks another question, but I can't seem to hear or remember it. He nods again.

"It's okay," he explains. "I know it's a lot to process at once. Let's just start from the beginning."

SIX

Once, when we were very young, Mother took us back to the place where she was born. A taxi came to take us to the airport, and we helped as best we could in the snow with the two suitcases, as well as the boxes Mom brought containing a toaster oven, a cassette radio, and two tins of maple syrup. I remember the taxi took us across the city in the winter traffic, and then the brightness of the airport, the ads everywhere for watches and cars and clothes and fancy dinners. I remember the long lineup with others carrying suitcases and boxes, and

Mother's confusion for a moment when she couldn't find the tickets, and all the while our own excitement and nervousness as we searched the faces of others behind us. Tourists, some of them. But others travelling "back" to that mysterious place that some—but never our mother—called home.

I don't remember much from the actual flight, only scattered sensations. I remember standing on the seat to put my hand through the stream of air flowing from above, and also flicking on and off an overhead light, Mother too tired to scold me twice. I remember complaining about my ears, and another passenger giving me minty adult gum, too strong to enjoy. I remember waiting to get out of the plane, and then walking into another airport. Around us were some of the very same ads for watches and cars and clothes that we had seen in that first airport at the start of the trip. The air in this second airport was cold, colder, it felt, than that wintry place we had left behind. And I worried if, somehow, we had been fooled. If, really, we hadn't travelled anywhere at all, or if the world were everywhere the same.

But when we stepped outside, it was hot. The sun had just begun to set, and we got into a car that was loud and smelled badly of exhaust even when we got moving. The driver might have been a relative, but I don't remember an introduction or a conversation. Around the airport, a field of sharp light pushed back at the surrounding darkness, and I could see billboards along the road show-ing nice places to stay, with the bluest waters and beaches of white sand. But as we kept driving, for hours it seemed, it became hard to see anything at all. I caught only the yellow orbs of street lamps and the ribbed metal top of a building, and then fewer street lamps, and finally little else but a great moon and the bright starry sky. There were the smells of flowers, thick in my nose and throat, and also mud and dung and decay.

Mother's family lived in a village named Ste. Madeleine, in the middle of the island, and the ride was very long and sick-winding. But finally we rocked upon the pot-holes of a dirt road and pulled up in front of a big single-storey house. There was scurry of a creature into the shadows, a reptilian tail, did you see that, I asked. But Mother was already out of the car to hug a woman who had stepped outside as soon as the car pulled up. Francis held my hand, and the first greeting that I received in that place of "back" or "home" was from a spotted dog, who lunged at us against a frayed rope, baring his teeth.

Everyone else in the house was asleep, and we were told there'd be proper introductions in the morning. Mother was to share a bed in another part of the house with the woman who had greeted her, her sister, and Francis and I were put to sleep together on a mat on the floor of the living room. We brushed our teeth at a pipe outdoors that offered only cold water. And trying to pee one last time before bed, I stepped on something hard but moving, an insect, prehistoric big it seemed to me, that clicked angrily and flapped away.

Francis and I lay down on our mat, but when the lights were turned off, we couldn't sleep. Wild creatures called in the dark, and the air was filled with the hum of insects, louder than any traffic we heard at home. The living room window framed a full moon that shone like a cool white sun, and billions of stars, a universe we had never even imagined. I remembered Mother would sometimes tell us tales of the ghosts and spirits that foolish little children walking alone in her birthplace might imagine themselves encountering. Of soucouyants and lagahoos. Of duennes, little children who died before baptism, before the proper rites could be performed, and who then would roam the wild and forested places, luring living children to their deaths. These stories were never meant to scare us, and they never really did. The names given to the creatures too strange to be truly fearful.

But during that first night in Mother's birthplace, I remember feeling afraid, though of what I did not know. Something old and unburied in the darkness, something closer to us now than ever before. I remember lying awake with Francis and hearing for the first time the scream of a rooster, my brother's hand pressed hard in mine. The sun still hadn't risen, and I remember looking at Francis, who lay beside me very still with his eyes wide open. I remember searching for a clue about our situation in some slight movement of his ear, or of his jaw, or of that expressive space between his mouth and nose. And when he caught me looking at him, he swallowed and nodded.

"Don't be afraid," he said.

In the morning, it was different. We met a blur of uncles and aunts and older cousins. We had a proper introduction to Nora, our mother's sister, heavier and older. We met a very old and skinny man with eye-whites that were brown, and he was my grandfather, and he never left his bed. We met another "aunt" of some uncertain connection to us named Beulah, with the sharpest eyes and a sore on her mouth that was disgusting, and that you also somehow wanted to touch. We met many "cousins," boys and girls of complicated relation to me and Francis, who looked the two of us up and down and who seemed never satisfied about our responses to any of their questions about "America."

What was this place of origins we had we come to? In the years to come, Francis and I would hear the words slavery and indenture. We'd learn that the Caribbean was named after people who'd been pushed by murder and disease to the very brink of oblivion.

But what of these histories could we read in the land we saw as children? Around us were wasted farmlands and abandoned cane fields, punctuated by what looked like shacks. We heard our poor black relatives speak of coolies, and our poor Indian relatives speak of niggers, and both sides huff laughter at "the Carib woman," our distant relative, who sold green seasoning at the market and was obviously half-mad. All of this somehow worked together with the modern airport we had come from and its ads for fine restaurants and hotels, or else the luxury cars and office buildings we'd spotted in the capital. The white beaches of advertisements were reserved for tourists of the proper sort, for the one we visited was small and rocky, the sand carrying a black stickiness and a tarry smell. There was a yellow foam in parts of the water that we were told to avoid, and Aunt Beulah told us that years ago a ship from overseas had left the oil refinery on the island and ground up against a rock and spilled much of its cargo.

But here too was beauty. The sea itself was fierce with light and colour. The hills were thick with the deepest green, and there were lizards and the brightest birds that made a joyous racket. And our relatives, on both sides of our family, were beautiful. These were people who could throw scorn at others in the most casual way and then also, in a moment, laugh. There was a souse that looked to us like garbage, and we shivered at the split head and the feet with gristly knobs of pink and white. But when we tasted it we wanted more. There was ice cream hand-cranked in a rock salt bath by a neighbour.

One night, we were taken to an old white church. We were greeted as "brethren" and ushered into the service. Inside were many candles, and people dressed in different colours. The preacher held a book, but rarely read from it. Instead, he pounded it expressively while the congregation shouted out in unknowable tongues. Something about redemption and the persecuted, something about Canaan and promised lands and how God gave everyone a secret name, the deep name that only he knew, and he would call you this one day, and you would answer fully.

I felt amazement at all of this, at the loud spectacle that I'd never seen before of adults, and when I looked to Francis for an explanation, I saw him looking on, listening to that strange language and music and noise with a wet face.

I remember, very clearly, the drive back to the airport. I remember Aunt Beulah wasn't asked to come with us, and that my mother's other sister sat in the car with us. She explained how sad she was that her sister and her boys were leaving. When would we return? When would my mom see her nephews and nieces again? She missed our mother's company and jokes. She missed the times they had travelled together to town for dances.

"And do you still like to dance, Ruth? Do you still go out dancing?"

"Sometimes," Mother told her, watching the fields passing by.

And in the quiet that followed, my aunt found the voice to make a confession. It had not been easy since Mother had left. And sometimes, explained my aunt, she had even been jealous of her older sister, and the perfect life that she alone had found by going away.

Mother stayed quiet. She did not say that our father had left us years before. She did not admit that she had not had the time or money to complete her studies to become a nurse. She did not hint at the debt or struggle or the aches she often felt. As we headed to the airport, she just nodded and looked out the window at the coconut trees towering black against the evening sky, and the old untended fields of cane stretching out like a sea.

It wasn't just "she alone." All around us in the Park were mothers who had journeyed far beyond what they knew, who took day courses and worked nights, who dreamed of raising children who might have just a little more than they did, children who might reward sacrifice and redeem a past. And there were victories, you must know. Fears were banished by the scents from simmering pots, denigration countered by a freshly laundered tablecloth.

History beaten back by the provision of clothes and yearly school supplies. "Examples" were raised.

Our mother, like others, wasn't just bare endurance and sacrifice. There was always more to her, pleasures and thoughts we could only glimpse. The times she visited her beauty salon, and how she leaned her hair back into a sink, her eyes closed in pleasure, another woman's hands in her hair. The time our neighbour Sonny Barrington put his arm around her and said something into her ear and made her laugh, a silly real laugh. The time we watched her spend a day on the couch with an amazingly thick library book. That whole day never once driving herself frantic with duty, just reading. Whole chapters of time spent in quiet aloneness. Reaching up in concentration to touch her own earlobe, to pinch it gently while something on the page stilled her.

And the Rouge. It was Mother, really, who introduced Francis and me to this place. When we were very little, she'd walk us down the rabbit path, and we'd eat on the grass beside the creek, ignoring the bugs and pushing away the stray dog we named Rudebwoy forever nosing us for company and food. We'd spend whole seasons of time down there. The falls when the valley floor was a bowl of yellow and orange and red. The winters when the trees were bare, the ice locking up the creek, our breath on the stillest days like purest calcium in the air before us. The summers when the creek shrank and the gooseberries along the side of the path broke at the slightest touch, insects bumbling about heavy and tired with pollen and nectar. And that magic spring, I still remember it, when the creek rushed extra fast and high with the winter melts. When there was everywhere the fluff of some plant in the air. White spores, millions of them, each of them a memory, a dream waiting to land and bloom.

Always, for our mother, there was the hidden life to point out for us in the Rouge. The monarchs she explained had crossed whole lands to be here. The bird of prey she spotted on the day after she and her co-workers were all suddenly let go, a red-shouldered hawk, pure fierceness and pride. Even once, on our way back home, a raccoon leaving a dumpster, tiptoeing unafraid with a queenly rump-high walk. She'd show us weeping willows and maples, that great father of trees with its corduroy bark welling with sap, a sea of sticky goodness for insects. Once she put a sprig of pine up to Francis's nose, smiling awkwardly when my brother named its peculiar smell.

"It's Mr. Clean!" he said.

What was the hope or philosophy in these excursions? What is a mother's dream of land? Once, when Francis had one of his nightmares, the terror overwhelming, impossible as always to name, Mother again took us to the Rouge. Lying in bed beside us, she told us with eyes closed and in a voice turned dreamlike with exhaustion of little moths that flocked and hovered around the ugly tufts of a plant at the creek's edge. And maybe, if you weren't watching the right way, you wouldn't even think they were moths when you saw them. You'd think they were just little bits of paper tossing and turning in the wind. As though someone took an old book and ripped it to bits and threw them up in the wind. Letters gone missing from each other. A scattered and wasted alphabet. Without any meaning at all . . .

"Mother?" asked Francis, looking at her with concern.

"But look closer," she said, eyes still closed. "Cup your hand and feel the proof of them against you. They're not trash. They're living things. And they're flying."

We never spoke as a family about what happened, once, when Francis and I were still very young. One afternoon, a group of young men entered a convenience store in a neighbourhood we didn't know and botched a robbery, shot a clerk and left him to die alone. But there was a security camera in the store, and grainy images of the murderers were broadcast throughout the city.

Mother was working a twelve-hour night shift, and so Francis and I sat alone at home watching those images of the shooters on the television. They moved in jerks, a frame count running at the bottom of the screen. They hunched into their big jackets, hands driven hard into their pockets, one pulling down the brim of his cap as he entered. There were no other telling details. Just fields of shadows. Murder reduced to three indistinguishable dark faces, haunting the city. In the very early morning, a newspaper was pushed into our mail slot, the subscription Mother had always insisted upon, even in tight times, and it featured on its front page the same images, but also, inside, a news story and even what I'd later understand as an editorial. Francis was seven at the time, and just beginning to learn how to read, just beginning to understand what is executed every day in language, and he studied the words surrounding the black faces. There was a growing fear in him that, sitting beside him, I smelled and felt, but that he would not express.

It was morning before Mother returned home, and Francis and I had still not gone to bed. Francis had put a chair up against the door for our safety, like he'd seen on TV. When Mother unlocked the door, though, she pushed it open slowly but easily.

"My boys," she said softly.

She came towards us on the couch. She sat on the armrest beside my brother and said she was sorry for being away so long, but Francis turned his face back towards the morning show on television as if the baking demonstrated on the screen was the most important thing in the world. I remember Mother gently rolling into a tight baton the very same newspaper Francis had read, and that she too had likely read on the way home. I remember her trying to touch Francis but my brother shifting away. She looked so tired. She smelled of sweat and detergents.

"Let me take you boys somewhere," she said.

We caught a bus and then a commuter train, and we arrived at a mall that was big and bright and had polished marble floors. All around us were fancy shops, selling clothing and cosmetics and showing life-sized images of beautiful people, a few with light brown faces. As we moved from store to store, the clerks seemed especially attentive to us. Mother hadn't changed out of her uniform, and her sneakers sounded her approach on the marble floors with a funny squeaking sound. Another clerk approached unsmilingly and said, "Can I help you?" "No thank you, just window shopping," Mother said brightly. We walked by a big sculpture of polished steel, and in it I caught our reflections and realized that Francis and I weren't looking our best either.

"No thanks, we're just window shopping," Mother explained again and again.

There was a cinema in the mall, and Mother took us to watch an action movie. It was the usual thing, lots of gunfire and flowing-haired heroism, explosions in some tropical setting, with the jeep of good guys speeding free. It all ended happily, but it somehow seemed to exhaust us, drive the air right out of our bodies. Afterwards, we were lucky to spot an empty table right underneath a wall-mounted television, and we scored it for ourselves amidst the bustle. Mom bought us hot dogs and Cokes and a cup of coffee for herself.

Nobody spoke. We had all missed a night of sleep, and everything that had happened to us now seemed to weigh heavily. My brother still wasn't speaking or meeting Mom's eyes. In the air around us were mysterious soft voices, and I was confused and even a bit panicked until I realized it was just a news update coming from the TV mounted above us. Mother held her styrofoam cup of coffee without drinking from it. Cradling it with both hands. As if drawing all her energy from its weak warmth. A thin skin of white floating on the surface.

There was an announcement on loudspeakers that the mall would be closing and that the food court would have to be cleared, but she didn't seem to hear. Three white boys had been looking at us.

"You're supposed to go now," one said. "They're closing the mall."

"We are preparing to go," said Mother.

"Hey," said the other boy. "He just told you. You're not supposed to be here anymore. You people better listen for once."

"Leave us alone," said Francis.

"Francis!" said Mother.

There was a smile from the boys. "*Francis,*" they repeated, smirking.

Francis stood and walked towards them, but he was easily pushed away, and he fell back hard on his bum. He got up and went to them again, but Mother pushed herself in between. The boys had their hands on her, grabbing her clothes and tugging and shoving for position and balance, and Francis and I started screaming. One of the boys seemed determined to put Mother in an arm lock, but she broke from it and slapped him hard. He held his cheek and finally backed away. "Nigger cunt," he said.

When the defenders of the mall were gone, Mother quickly smoothed her uniform and patted her hair. She brushed at the streak of dirt on Francis's shirt, and she held each of our faces.

"A couple punks, that's all," she said, and tried to smile.

When we got home, Mother made butter sandwiches for everyone, but nobody was hungry, and afterwards, for the first time ever, none of us felt like watching TV. We got into our pyjamas, and at last Francis's resentment melted away.

He asked Mother to stay with us, and she allowed us both to lay beside her on the bottom bunk, sharing her warmth although she still smelled of the previous night's work. It was a smell faint and vague but never-theless there, not only of sweat and the throat rot of exhaustion and missed meals, not only of the vapours of chemicals on her skin and in her hair, but something else. Something old, forever clinging. She stroked our heads, and she began telling us one of her stories set long ago and in a different land, a legend this time about children who were lured into a forest by wicked little creatures, but she kept stopping, kept losing track of the tale she wanted to tell. "I'm sorry, I'm so tired, I can't remember, I can't go on." She stood and asked Francis to return to his top bunk and then she turned off the light. I lay there with Francis in the dark. That first dark since the shooting.

I tried closing my eyes, but dreamed, as maybe Francis did too, of those wanted men, their formless dark faces. Outside the trees were clawed with ice and the wind blew and rattled the windows and brushed sleet on the panes.

A shout from outside. The gunning of some powerful machine on the avenue.

Francis climbed down from his bunk and helped me up from my own and led me down the hallway towards Mother's bedroom. Mother wasn't sleeping, she hadn't even changed out of her uniform. She was just sitting on her bed in the dark. Her face turning towards us.

"He's afraid," Francis said, touching me.

"Come here. What is he afraid of?"

"I don't know. Maybe the black murderers."

"The . . . *who*?"

"The murderers. In the news. The black men . . ."

She closed her eyes, pressed her temples. She recovered. "The *criminals*, Francis. The *criminals* will be caught by the police and punished. They do not stand a chance. Please try to understand. We're lucky here. We're very safe."

"He doesn't believe we're very safe."

"We *are*, Francis."

"We're not. We never were."

"You are confused and tired. You must please, *for me*, calm down."

"You're not telling him the truth."

"Yes I am, Francis."

"I don't believe you."

"But I *need* you to believe me."

She was gripping him by the arm and shaking him. Pain upon his face but sudden terror when he met her eyes. Mother touched her face, realized she was crying.

"What happened?" asked Raj. "Can someone just tell me? Who did this?"

I had run after Francis and caught up with him just outside the strip mall, passing shopkeepers arriving in the dark for work and now staring at the bloodied young man. I helped him into Desirea's and the boys joined me at once and got him into a barber's chair. For a moment, they stood staring too. But suddenly Dru was doing what he could with gauze and medical tape. Francis was uncooperative. He seemed drunk, shifting around and talking to himself.

"Sit still, homeboy," Dru said. "Just a little longer."

"I don't get it," said Raj, turning to Jelly. "You said it happened at the audition? Were you jumped?"

Jelly didn't answer. Dru managed to patch up some of the ragged flesh on Francis's face, blooms of red showing through the bandages. When he tried to touch another wound with alcohol on a cloth, Francis cursed and jerked away.

"Easy, homeboy," said Dru. "You've got to calm down."

"He needs a hospital," said Jelly. "His eyes . . . his pupils don't match."

Francis rose unsteadily from his chair and started towards Raj, but Dru stepped in the way, telling him gently that he needed to sit. Jelly said the same, touching his arm. Francis swayed at bit, glaring at Raj.

"What's your problem?" said Raj, carefully.

"What's *my* problem?" said Francis. "*Look* at yourself. Look at all of you."

Raj blinked, looked at Jelly and Dru, looked around at the others all up on their feet now. Trance, Kev, Raj, Dru. Gene. Had I recognized it only then? We were losers and neighbourhood schemers. We were the children of the help, without futures. We were, none of us, what our parents wanted us to be. We were not what any other adults wanted us to be. We were nobodies, or else, somehow, a city.

"We're all just dreaming," Francis said. "It wasn't ever going to work."

"Homeboy," said Jelly, pulling him down.

"Nobody's listening. There's no way forward."

Jelly didn't answer my brother in words. He didn't argue. He just touched him, stroked his back and neck. He held my brother's face and rested his forehead on his.

They were still touching when the cops showed up, and on one of the uniformed men was a look, a curled lip. There were many cops this time, more than the last time, and they were geared up, sweating in their vests. One announced that they were responding to a call from a shopkeeper, something about a fight, a boy badly injured, and Dru began explaining that nothing was going on. The cop pointed at Francis.

"What happened to him?"

"Nothing," said Dru. "He's just hurt. We're handling it."

"Okay," said the cop. "I want to see ID from everyone. Stand back near the wall, all of you. You know the drill."

"Come on, Fran," said Jelly.

He tried to get Francis up from the chair, and I helped too, although my brother's limbs were now stiff. He was clearly in pain and as he got to his feet he swore and pulled his arms away from us. He kicked the little metal stand where Dru kept his clippers and scissors. It toppled noisily to the ground.

"You three," said the cop, "stand apart."

"He's hurt," explained Jelly. "We're helping him up."

"We'll handle that. You do as we say."

"What did we do?" shouted Francis, his voice cracking.

He shook off our hands, struggled to stand, and he took a wobbled step forward to steady himself. Even to my eyes, he was a sight. He had broken into a sweat with the new pain. He coughed and spat something from his mouth, but badly, something thick and stringy clinging to his lip. I saw a cop undo his holster.

"You sit back down, sir," the cop said.

"Do it now," said Dru.

"Do it *now*," said Gene, her voice lowered.

"No," Francis said. "You tell me. What did we do?"

He stumbled with stiff limbs.

"Stay where you are," I heard a cop say. "Don't come any closer." Another clasp was taken off a holster. And when a gun was drawn, I got vertigo, the world spinning around the weapon. I couldn't move. Jelly still hadn't listened, he hadn't left Francis's side, but Francis was pushing ahead with him, pushing closer to the cop who had commanded. My brother was trembling, but there was an energy in him that wouldn't be stilled. His eyes had begun to grow wet, and as he smiled a scab broke open on his lip and streaked red upon his teeth.

"You think I'm crazy," he said. "You think I'm dangerous."

"I think I want you to sit down, sir," said a cop.

"Don't call me sir. Don't go around pretending anymore. You answer my question. You give me an explanation."

"We're not asking you a second time," a cop said.

"Do what he says," another cop said.

"Fran," said Jelly. "Please."

My brother stumbled once more. His eyes were bleeding water. His smile grew. "It's happening today," he said. "You're going to tell me what I've done."

"Don't move."

"*Now*. Not later."

"Do. Not. Move."

"Francis," I whispered.

I think I said this. I think I said his name. I'd seen a cop grab Jelly's arm. "Don't *touch* him," Francis said, and it was over. I don't even remember hearing the shot. My brother just fell.

SEVEN

It's early morning in the emergency ward, and a nurse has just updated me on Mother. Physically, there's nothing more serious than the hairline fracture of her femur. The car was likely slowing down when it struck her, and she is reasonably healthy. She's been given something strong for the pain, and so she may not be able to fully communicate just yet. In a short while, the doctor will be around to offer final updates before her release. The nurse can't say exactly when. It has been an unusually busy night, she explains. There have been other pressing cases.

I know about one of them. A couple hours ago, a boy was rushed in on a stretcher to the station across from us. He was unconscious, his head and neck in some stabilizing device. Two others came with him. A boy, probably his brother, wearing the sort of bomber jacket every kid around twelve seems to wear these days. A woman too, definitely his mother, dressed professionally in a skirt and white blouse. The boy on the stretcher was quickly hooked up to monitors, an oxygen mask applied to his face, a second IV started, while the nurses and doctors asked questions. His age again, ma'am? Medications taken? Known allergies? The mother had the voice of someone who uses it with authority, and also a vague Caribbean accent, but her voice wavered and her answers were hesitant, her eyes riveted only upon her son. A nurse with a clipboard asked the mother for an address, if she happened to have any ID for her son, preferably a health card, and the mother suddenly sharpened, pronounced it clearly.

"He is a citizen."

The nurse tapped the drip of the intravenous, checked on vitals. A doctor arrived with news of the X-rays, and he tried to reassure the mother. Her son had sustained a concussion, but no more serious head trauma. He had a broken collarbone, but his back and neck were apparently all right, and he would recover.

"I have to ask," said the doctor. "Why on earth were you boys up on the roof of your house at night?"

"To see," the younger brother admitted softly.

Now, behind the light blue drape, I hear the mother speaking discreetly into her phone. "Yes, he's all right. Yes, he's very lucky." And it's true, for this family at least. Sure as day, there'll be scolding and punishment, but no funeral. No "complicated grief," no greater meaning in this everyday accident. Just two boys hoping to see.

ON THE MORNING OF FRANCIS'S FUNERAL, Mother and I took a long time getting dressed. I did the buttons on my shirt wrongly and stared at my mistake failing to understand it for what seemed a full minute. Mother ironed her black dress so slowly I smelled the fabric burning. She fixed her hair in front of the bathroom mirror, redoing her work at least three times, and she must have applied her Chantilly perfume more than once, forgetting the times before, because the smell of it filled the cab as we travelled to the funeral home. Mother turned to me, asked me in a whisper if I'd remembered to turn the lights off. I said yes and tried to read her face as she touched her temple with a dampened tissue.

"Did you put on clean socks?" she asked.

Mrs. Henry was there, in a midnight-purple hat, no doubt reserved for occasions like these. Dru was there, of course, and also the Professa, Gene, Raj, Kev, even little Trance. A day before, they had come as a group to our door, and when I answered there was awkward quiet before Dru cleared his throat. "We would like to offer our condolences," he said. I couldn't even say thank you. I just nodded and closed the door, and now they just nodded at me from their seats, in their borrowed suits either too tight or too big. They looked so stiff and quiet, so unlike the boys I knew. Jelly wasn't among them. When Francis was shot he wouldn't stop scream-ing and struggling, he had been charged with resisting arrest, and he still hadn't posted bail.

Aisha was there, with her father. The day before, she too had tried to visit me. I'd opened the door and dropped my eyes when I saw it was her. She had moved to hug me, and I'd flinched so strongly that it startled us both. I'd told her it wasn't a good time, and I'd closed the door and didn't open it the second and third time she knocked. Now I felt her eyes upon me, and it became convenient for me to look elsewhere in the room. In a seat near the back, away from others, I noticed a man in a well-fitting tan suit.

He might have been one of those people in the Park who made a strange habit of going to funerals. But there was something about this man; he seemed somehow familiar, but I couldn't place him. I didn't want to stare, but I studied his earlobes, which I suddenly wanted to touch as proof. He noticed me looking, and nodded.

It was a simple Pentacostal ceremony, arranged by Mrs. Henry, and the pastor was thoughtful with his words and kind in his acknowledgement of Mother and me. After a hymn that I never really heard, the service was over.

I remember helping Mother to rise to sign some papers. And I remember watching, mesmerized by the time she took with the script, the immense and terrible care, the elegant loops at the beginning of her name, at the beginning of the month, the perfect even slant of the letters, a crossed *t*, a dotted *i*.

When I looked again, the man in the tan suit was gone.

When Francis and I were young, as small a matter as a spot of food on our shirts, or a crust of toothpaste around our mouths, could raise fury in our mother. "You don't listen!" she might shout at us. "You all don't pay attention to what I tell you. You all is *harden*! Too too *harden*." If we ever hurt ourselves, she would promise to "corn our backsides." She vowed to whip the life force back into us if ever through sheer foolishness we cut ourselves and shamefully bled our lives away. And after Francis's death, and in the terrible quiet and composure that now set upon her, I hoped she would find that threatened rage, even if she directed it towards me. A rage that, I knew, wouldn't ever rouse Francis back to life, but might do that for her.

The rage did not come. And on the cab ride home from the funeral, Mother sat as still as before. We returned to our door at the Waldorf, and she retrieved a bill from the mailbox and placed it carefully on the kitchen table as she always did to remind herself to pay it. The weather had begun to cool, but our place was still hot. She went to her bedroom to lie down, and I checked on her at least a couple times, putting a wet cloth on her forehead. Her eyes were opened each time, but she never spoke.

She didn't get up again until evening, and after forcing down some crackers at my insistence, she started tidying. She fetched a broom and swept the kitchen, attacking the hard-to-reach crack between the fridge and the wall. She recovered cobwebs and hair, greeting cards, crystallized bits of orange rind, the emptied shells of insects. She washed the few dishes left in the sink, and then retrieved an already clean baking pan from its drawer under the stove and attacked it with steel wool, scrubbing for a long time.

"I'll be back soon," I told her, leaving behind me the harsh sounds of her work.

It was by this time getting close to twilight, and as

I walked the street lamps came on. I visited the playground where I had spent time with Aisha, now a nighttime scene of lights and shadows. I made wide circles around the Park at least five times, and I crossed the Lawrence Avenue bridge. I was disoriented, light-headed with having not eaten all day, and when I stared down into the unseen depths of the great glacial valley, it felt like I could fall. A transport trailer flew past, its wake pulling and pushing me like a flimsy non-living thing. I gripped the edge of the bridge for balance, and this steadied me back to life.

A bird of some sort, maybe a pigeon, clattered the bridge, trying to find a place to roost on its underside. It tried to gain a foothold but slipped and smacked its wings a few more times against the concrete before giving up. It flapped up above street level and across the middle floors of a high-rise before flying in the direction of my home.

I hadn't left Mother alone for this long since Francis's death, and I started hurrying with concern even before I spotted the small crowd of neighbours grouped outside our unit. I stopped in their midst, awaiting an explanation, but none was offered. A vague anxiety in the air.

"Mrs. Henry . . . ?" I began.

"Your mother," she said.

And then I heard it. A loud bump coming from inside our unit. The creak and dull scrape of something being moved about in the living room. A shattering, things spilling on the floor, sharp little bullets of sound.

Another bump. A clatter of something metal hitting the floor.

I pushed open the door slowly, the security chain dangling. It was stifling hot and at first I couldn't make out much from the white shock of light of the fridge left open, but I could tell all the furniture had been moved. The couch and chairs had been pushed to the edges, the rug rolled sloppily and stood up in a corner. The kitchen table had been moved, its chairs on their sides.

She was kneeling by the couch, a hammer in her hand, banging at something, her face turned away from me. I called her name. Her eyes wide at me in the dark. These really wide eyes. All the drawers and cupboards in the kitchen area were yawning empty, and the few canned and boxed things within had been piled on the linoleum, garbage sweepings, broken glass and dishes, pairs of good shoes.

"It's such a mess," she explained.

"Mother. Please," I whispered.

"Who leaves their home in such a mess?"

From that moment, Mother became someone I could care for. I had the everyday urgencies of watching her, making sure she ate and tried to sleep. She became a convenient excuse when people came to visit or to try to offer condolences, and when the boys from Desirea's returned again to speak with me, I could angrily explain that they were disturbing us. They never returned.

Even the police interview about the death of my brother could seem to me, right then, a distraction, a conversation too late and somehow all beside the point. Mother was forced to come with me because I was still not quite eighteen, and we both sat dazed and nodding at the questions asked by those in authority. Could I clarify on the words exchanged in the shop that day? Could I remember the precise language used? Could I help affirm what others had already described as the actions leading up to the discharge of the weapon? I nodded, not always able to listen. I kept looking at my mother, this first excursion for her since the funeral. She was staring down at the tea that she had been given, growing cold now in her hands. She refused to meet anyone's eyes, to be moved by anything discussed or said in this room.

What else happened? I remember the buzzing of the fluorescent lights, and that the air conditioning was cranked, encasing us, finally, in cold. I remember the silences in that room much more than the talk. But also their questions. Would you agree that Francis had a bit of a reputation? Did he sometimes exhibit unpredictable moods? Would you agree, Michael, that your brother possessed a history of violence?

———

There was Aisha, of course. She came to see us again, but when I began to close the door she jammed her foot and then pushed her way in. She set bags of food on the kitchen counter, two of them, smelling spiced and peppery, the paper stained almost translucent with grease. Roti, no doubt. I explained that Mother was sleeping, explained that we couldn't speak. I explained that the smell of food nauseated me, and she nodded.

"The library," she said.

We walked to it in silence, and when I entered the building, I felt the attention. I must have looked like crap, I hadn't showered in days, and there were stares, but Aisha didn't seem to care. She led us to our usual seats, and she asked how Mother was doing. She asked how I was doing. I nodded, and she waited before trying again. She said that she'd tried to contact the boys from Desirea's. She'd tried to find out what had happened. What had *really* happened. Most of the boys had fled, and the few remaining had nothing to say. Jelly had been released, but he'd vanished into the city.

"This can't be the end," she said. "We still need to talk."

I looked away from her. Around us were people reading, a girl looking into a computer screen, her face painted blue by the light.

Francis had always protected me. It was his instinct.

He saw the vulnerability, understood it all too well. But in that final moment in Desirea's, he had tried to protect another. When a cop with his hand on his holstered gun grabbed Jelly and tried to pull him away, Francis had panicked. "Don't touch him," he'd said, reaching to still the weapon. It was a gesture with history, but unreadable by those around him holding power. The authorities had investigated, interviewed witnesses, pronounced their conclusions.

"They called it lawful," I told Aisha. And what else could we do but each look away?

There are many ways a person can flee. Aisha left for university. And my brother's friends each, in their own ways, fled. But of course, you can't ever really flee. You'll forever run the risk of being spotted, if only for a second. Once, a couple years after the shooting, reaching for juice in the refrigerator of a convenience store, I noticed a young man reaching too, and when our eyes met, he nodded, the sort of nod that says not only excuse me but also I see you, I recognize. And only after he had left, I realized it was Kev. A year or two later, someone on a bus looked up at me from her newspaper, that awkward look of memory on the face before me. Gene. Years after Desirea's was reopened as the second Happy Chicken in the neighbourhood, I was leaving a drugstore with a prescription for Mother when a man held the door open for me. At first he pretended not to see or know me, but as I stepped through the doorway, he swallowed and said, "Hey, Michael. You okay?" He wore a suit jacket, the kind they make you wear in retail. And his name tag didn't say "Raj," or "Rajinder," but "Hello, I'm Roddy."

Last summer, Dru knocked on the door. He was visiting his sister, still in the neighbourhood, and beside him was a boy of maybe five, his son, the fattest eyes you've ever seen, although already he could posture, chinning me a quick hello in a way that made me laugh. We spent an hour together in the nearby Tim Hortons, drinking those slushy coffee drinks, beads of cold on their plastic cups. I ordered a doughnut for his son, and I kept watching, mesmerized, as the kid forked off all the icing to eat first. We joked just a bit about Desirea's, but when I asked Dru if he ever thought of opening another shop, he shook his head. "This one keeps me busy," he said, gesturing at his boy. He asked me carefully about my mother, and when I said, "She's getting better," he tried his best to return my smile. We finished our coffees and Dru said he had to get back to his sister's, he had the kid to feed, and, you know, other responsibilities.

"I understand," I said.

"You take care, Michael. Okay?"

I said I would. I had my own responsibilities. I had my mother, and I had my job. I had free time at the library. I have lived, just like others, which is something.

Not long before Aisha's return, I was sitting in the library when I heard a man say, "Do you mind?" I shifted away from the empty chair beside me, my eyes still on the page of my book. When I noticed the man was taking a long time to lower himself into his seat, I turned to look. Like other neighbours, Aisha's father had tried to offer his condolences when Francis was killed, but he had respected my obvious desire for space, and we never spoke further. But now, as I looked at him, he seemed suddenly to have aged, his skin crinkled, his hair come out in patches. I'd heard rumours that he wasn't doing well, but I didn't expect this. We both pretended to read but kept catching each other's eyes. And eventually Samuel put down his book.

He told me that he had wanted to speak with me for a long time, and that he was sorry that he hadn't done so earlier. He was moving away soon, he might not have another chance to speak. He just wanted me to know that in the months before Francis died, perhaps a year or more, he and Francis had met to listen to music. It began one day when he was returning from work, passing by Francis while humming an old tune under his breath, and Francis just as quietly named the song. "Ne Me Quitte Pas," this youth of the Park had somehow managed to pronounce. After a moment of quiet, Samuel surprised himself by inviting Francis over to listen to

173

his records, and even more surprisingly, Francis had showed up a couple days later.

"We ended up spending only a few afternoons together, just listening to old music. Barely even talking. We must have played Nina Simone's version of 'Ne Me Quitte Pas' at least a dozen times. Her sweet sad voice. He always laughed, your brother, whenever I tried to sing that song. It became our joke. Our secret too, I think. I'm not sure if even Aisha knew. How could we explain it to others? A man like me, a boy like Francis. Who would have guessed at a connection?"

I could picture Francis sitting with a father, though not *his* father, listening together to Nina Simone and maybe Otis Redding and Sam Cooke. I could imagine, too, on a later visit, when the mood and sound were right, Francis telling something to this father who was not his father. A declaration that he, my brother, understood the old music, that heritage of love, because he felt it himself. He loved his family, and also his friends. He loved a young man named Jelly.

I must have worn something like embarrassment on my face. This vision I'd allowed myself. Fantasy more than memory. Samuel might have read my expression, and maybe he too felt embarrassed for whatever he had now attempted, because he chose then to rise unsteadily to leave.

"He died two weeks ago," Aisha told me over the phone, that day before her return. "He'd been staying in a hospice in Milton, and I didn't know. He never told me. He never said."

There was quiet on the phone. Not quite silence: someone breathing.

"Please visit," I said. "Come home to the Park."

It's morning now, and in a section of the emergency ward a distance away from Mother, the doctor is privately delivering the official diagnosis. The preliminary assessments hold up. Aside from the bruised ribs and hairline fracture, there's nothing else wrong with her. There was a high blood alcohol count, he continues, which may have contributed to disorientation when attempting to cross the street. A simple mistake, most likely, although there remains the question of her psychological state. She will need a support network. Has she been taking medicine? Do you have a family physician? I nod at the last question, lying.

When he leaves, I close my eyes. In the books on complicated grief, there are sometimes frank words. Some deaths, they explain, will never simply be "gotten over." Some mourners will never quite again "be themselves." I spend a good half-hour alone, haunting a hallway of the hospital, until I notice I'm making some visitors uncomfortable. I return to Mother's stretcher, and she's sitting up now, wearing a hospital gown as neatly as she can make it seem. When she reads my face, she smooths her hair, sits up straight, the paper beneath her making soft crinkling sounds.

"It is a new day," she says firmly.

I give her the space and privacy to put on her clothes, helping her only with the buttons of her blouse at the end. I borrow a wheelchair, although Mother is reluctant to sit in it, and we wheel carefully through the emergency ward to the main entrance where we can catch a bus. Shifts are changing from night to day, and passing us are cleaners and nurses' assistants and security guards. We pass the first window we've seen in hours, and Mother is right, it is a new day. It's bright outside.

In the atrium, I'm surprised to see them. And then somehow not surprised. They're precisely the sort to ignore a command to go away. They are exactly what my mother would call *harden*.

Aisha rises when she sees us, and she taps Jelly, who does the same, carrying a very small bunch of flowers in his hand. They are blue and pretty and wild.

"Can we visit it soon?" Aisha asks. "It's supposed to be warm this weekend."

We're all at home now, the four of us, and the room is filled with the smell of a fish poached in garlic and onions. Mrs. Henry has dropped off fruit and hard-dough bread, and Jelly has been improvising again in the kitchen. I'm having seconds of a bitter green that is delicious, fried rice with each grain sitting miraculously on its own. We have eaten, and there is music low on the record player, and we are here and for the moment together.

"What do you say?" Aisha presses. "The pathway down should be clear enough to get close to the creek. We'll be sure to go slow, Ruth. Maybe we could borrow a wheelchair. Jelly? Are you in?"

He nods from the record player, flipping through Mother's old albums, selecting one and checking for scratches. He cues it up, and when the low voice of a woman cuts the silence, Mother frowns slightly, as if in pain. Jelly fumbles to dial it down, but Mother shakes her head. Gestures upward.

"Volume," she says.

ACKNOWLEDGEMENTS

> Decide,
> Will you share the labor, share the work?
> —*Antigone*

> I don't remember that frail morning,
> how could I?
> —Dionne Brand, *Thirsty*

This short book took me a long time to write. I have benefitted profoundly from the editorial acuity of Martha Kanya-Forstner and the professional guidance of Jackie Kaiser. My warm thanks also to Jared Bland, Lara Hinchberger, Terri Nimmo, and Shaun Oakey. I must especially acknowledge the inspiring faith of the late Ellen Seligman.

I am grateful to all my friends. But for essential feedback on this book, I thank Phanuel Antwi, Darcy Ballantyne,

Wayde Compton, Kyo Maclear, Leslie Sanders, Madeleine Thien, Ian Williams, and Lise Winer. For advice on specific details, I thank Michael Bucknor, Daniel Coleman, Colette Colligan, Brady Cranfield, Janet Fitzsimmons, Kelly Josephs, Christine Kim, Michelle Levy, Stephen Murray, Beth Piatote, and Deanna Reder.

The Vancouver Public Library provided me with free space to write. A grant from the Canada Council for the Arts allowed me a precious break from teaching. The Banff Centre and the Literary Colloquium Berlin offered me short retreats. I am honoured by the interest and good wishes of my students and colleagues at Simon Fraser University.

I acknowledge the Indigenous lands that I live upon. I acknowledge the many stories that remain to be heard.

I am here and able to write because of the journeys, labours, and love of my parents, Rawlins and Claudette. I am grateful for the kindness and hospitality of my extended family. I am sustained by the wisdom of my brother, Mark, and by the creativity of my children, Maya and Skye.

For companionship in the weather, I thank Dionne Brand, Abdi Ousman, Christina Sharpe, and Rinaldo Walcott. A special thanks, once more, to Leslie Sanders. My deepest, heartfelt gratitude goes to my partner and first reader, Sophie McCall.

Austin Clarke believed in me. Thank you, Austin. Rest in peace.

A NOTE ON THE AUTHOR

David Chariandy grew up in Toronto and lives and teaches in Vancouver. His debut novel, *Soucouyant*, was nominated for nearly every major literary prize in Canada. It was shortlisted for the Governor General's Literary Award, won a Gold Independent Publisher Award for Best Novel and was longlisted for the Scotiabank Giller Prize. *Brother*, his second novel, was longlisted for the Scotiabank Giller Prize and won the Rogers Writers' Trust Fiction Prize.